I GOT YOUR *Back* 2

A NOVEL BY

SHVONNE LATRICE

© *2017*

Published by Shvonne Latrice

Presents

www.theshvonnelatrice.com

ALL RIGHTS RESERVED

Any unauthorized reprint or use of the material is prohibited. No part of this book may be reproduced or transmitted in any form or by any means, electronic, or mechanical, including photocopying, recording, or by any information storage without express permission by the publisher.

This is an original work of fiction. Names, characters, places and incidents are either products of the author's imagination or are used fictitiously and any resemblance to actual persons, living or dead is entirely coincidental.

Contains explicit language & adult themes suitable for ages 16+

$18.99

ISBN 978-1-966375-22-7

51899>

CHAPTER ONE

Tatiana

I went to the drugstore and once I returned I darted up the stairs and went into the bathroom. I retrieved the pregnancy tests from the paper bag, and just stared at them for a second. I'd been pregnant two times before, so I knew the symptoms and I had them. I had no idea what Teflon would think about us having a baby, but an abortion was not an option. Losing two children had made me desperate in a sense to become a mother, and at this point I didn't really care if the father was around.

"Here we go," I sighed, pulling my underwear down and peeing on the stick. I peed on the other one as well to make sure, and then set them on a paper towel before washing my hands.

I left out of the bathroom and sat on the edge of the bed to keep my mind off of the test while the few minutes needed passed. As I text Jadynn, and Groove's girlfriend Cecily, Brevin burst into the room. He stared me down for a few, and then leaned down to peck me gently.

"I'm sorry about earlier, I'm just dealing with some shit."

"I know," I nodded with a half smile.

He blew out hot air as he removed his hoodie, and then headed towards the bathroom in my room. It didn't dawn on me that I had my tests in there until he slammed the door closed. I hopped up to rush over, not even sure of what I'd planned to say, and by the time I got there he'd snatched the door open, wearing the angriest expression I'd ever seen on him. Looking down, I spotted the tests clutched tightly in his hands.

"How the fuck you pregnant Tati when I ain't been fucking you huh?" He stepped out of the bathroom towards me, and pulled his gun out, removing the safety.

"Those are old!" I yelled once he put the gun in my face. I didn't know what to say and it was the only thing I could think of. I figured by the time I started showing, which was around five months last time, Teflon and I would be together; well out in the open together.

"Why the fuck you got them all over the fucking counter then?"

"Because I wanted to see them! Not everybody can just get over me losing the baby as quickly as you can, Brevin! You never cared!"

"Baby," his tone softened as he placed his gun down on the dresser. "I'm sorry, I've just been losing my mind lately. And when I saw those tests, I just—"

"You have some nerve, when you got another woman pregnant, Brevin."

"Man I don' told you that ain't my damn baby, Tatiana!"

"Aye is everything okay in here," Teflon came into the bedroom.

I smiled on the inside, knowing that even though he was supposed to turn the other cheek he couldn't help it.

"Yeah man I'm just talking to *my* girl."

Staring Brevin hard in the eyes, Teflon didn't respond for a minute. Finally, he nodded his head coolly, and then left the bedroom.

"Brevin—"

"That nigga acts like he wants to fuck you or something!"

"No, he's just a protective person and he wants to make sure that nothing happens to me like the last time you went off."

"Well I'm gonna have a talk with him because I don't need nobody protecting you but me."

"And who is gonna protect me when I need protection from you." I touched the side of his handsome face.

I really wished we could have split amicably, because I knew this would end with him being dead, but this was his fault ultimately. The only way he would live is if he let me go willingly, and that was not going to happen.

"You don't need protection from me anymore. I'm gonna get my shit together." His arms circled my waist as he pulled me in. As his lips touched mine, I froze up, prompting him to pull away and frown. "Don't be scared of me, Tati. Things are gonna be different."

"Okay." I inhaled and exhaled sharply. "What would you like for dinner?" I removed his hands from my body. "I'm gonna go get my nails done at Cecily's shop, and then I'm gonna stop by the store."

"Aww shit," he grinned, and I smiled too since his was contagious despite the horrible person that he was. "Umm aight, steak, macaroni, and broccoli. Oh can you make an upside down pineapple cake too?"

"Of course."

"I love you ma." He pulled me in and leaned down to kiss my lips. This time I didn't jump, and let him do his thing. If I wanted things to go smoothly, I needed to play the part well. "I should be back well before dinner."

"Okay."

He kissed me once again but on the neck, and I watched him lock his gun back into his waist and leave the bedroom. Rushing to the bathroom, I picked up the pregnancy tests off the floor, and placed them into a Ziploc bag so I could show Teflon. When I came out of the bedroom, I saw he was leaving with Brevin and Merce, but not before he looked up at me. He gave me a wink, which made me feel all warm inside, just before he left out.

After slipping my shoes on, I grabbed my purse and phone, then left out to meet Jadynn at Cecily's nail bar.

***

I made it to Cecily's nail bar in no time, and saw Jadynn was already being worked on by Cecily's assistant, Ali. Jadynn and I were picky, so we only let Cecily or Ali touch our nails and eyebrows. I leaned down to kiss her cheek, and then took a seat next to her so Cecily could start on me.

"So how are things?" Cecily smiled as she began to place my hands in solution to remove the acrylic nails.

"They're good."

"Ryan told me you and Brevin have made up. I'm glad to see that's going well."

"Yes very well. I'm pretty happy," I chuckled along with Jadynn who was listening in. "How are things with you and Ryan?"

"Good, he's been working a lot more though since his childhood friends moved out here. You know, the ones that work for Brevin."

"Teflon and Merce."

"Yeah them. I hate that he works more, but I've noticed his spirit is much happier now that they're back so I don't complain."

"Ryan is a good guy," I assured her about Groove. I met him through Brevin even though he was Teflon's cousin, and so far he seemed to be a great guy. He was always trying to steer Brevin in the right direction, and I appreciated that back when I cared.

"I know and I keep reminding myself of that when I want to wring his neck for staying out at the damn club all night," she laughed.

I could tell she was bothered by something, but I'd wait to ask her that when the three of us were alone. I'm sure her employees would love to be in her business, and I refused to give them that.

The next two and a half hours flew by as Jadynn and I got pampered in Cecily's shop. Afterwards it was her lunchtime, so the three of us decided to go to Crop Bistro to get some food. Once we were seated, our waiter brought over some waters and took our order for an appetizer before prancing off.

"I guess now that we're away from the crowd I should give you the real deal," I spoke up and Cecily looked from me to Jadynn.

"Real deal on what?"

"Brevin and I. I'm leaving him."

"Oh my gosh, my prayers have been answered. When so I can help you pack up all of your shit?" She grinned.

"Soon. I'm gonna be with Teflon."

She started choking since I spoke when she had just sipped her water. When she got herself together, she inhaled and exhaled sharply.

"Where the hell have I been? You mean to tell me that you're leaving Brevin's no good ass for Ryan's little homie?"

"Nothing little about him," I smiled. I glanced at Jadynn who was quiet as a church mouse, so I knew she was trying to keep her budding relationship with Merce under wraps.

"Oooh girl. I'm happy for you even though I feel like what you're doing is dangerous."

"I know, and it is but it will work out. Now Jadynn, your turn."

"Huh?" Jadynn cheesed. Cecily and I both stared at her, so she sucked her teeth and sighed. "Well you already know about Russell and Paige, so that's over between him and I. But I kind of have something going on with Merce."

"Y'all two bitches are sneaky as fuck."

"No, you just need to get out more when we ask you to, and you would have known all of this."

"I know, I know. It's just after work I be so damn tired, and then taking care of Rye and his daddy bleeds me dry. But fuck that, I'm gonna start living again."

"You should."

I exhaled thinking about Teflon and the baby we would be having. If I could fast forward past all of this shit we were about to go through with Brevin, I would.

I Got Your Back 2

CHAPTER TWO

Teflon

Merce and I sat on opposite sides of Brevin as he discussed the moves he was currently making, and the ones he was about to make. He thought Merce and I were just here and not paying attention to shit, but little did he know, we were soaking that shit up like a couple of sponges.

"So this nigga from Jamaica has some good shit, and I'm thinking about flying out there or having him come here so we can talk. I've been slacking so I need to come back hard," Brevin explained.

The guy he was meeting with was some dude named Carnie, and I had never heard of or seen this nigga before in my life. I wasn't sure where Brevin had dug his ass up from, but I didn't care. Long as he didn't get in the way of the plans Merce, Groove, and I had for Brevin we'd be good. However, if he decided to step to me, his ass would be on the chopping block too.

"Damn word? Whatever you need help with I got you. Right now, Wade is taking shit over but I think you getting that Jamaican shit will help for sure."

Carnie and Brevin talked some more, and over the course of the conversation, I picked up that Carnie was basically Brevin's connection to the streets. He hung around niggas and played spy, only to run back to Brevin and tell. That shit had me feeling some type of way because I wondered if he would come across the fact that Tatiana and I were dating, or even worse, that we planned to take Brevin out. Granted, no one really knew but Merce, Groove, Tatiana, Jadynn, and I, but stranger things have happened.

Leaving out, the three of us piled into the big black Chevy Suburban that Brevin liked to travel in. Merce and I alternated when it was time to drive, and this time it was my turn. Glancing in my rearview mirror, I saw Brevin looking at me like he wanted to say something, and since I didn't like his ass and low-key wanted some confrontation with him, I decided to see what was up.

"You good my nigga?" I looked through the rearview. I could see Merce look to me as he sat in the passenger seat.

"Actually nah. I wanted to talk to you about me and Tatiana."

"What about y'all?"

"I need you to remember that she's my girl, and I don't need you looking out for her like you be trying to do."

"Wait, my job is to make sure nobody fucks with you, yet you want me to not do the same for your woman?"

I hated hearing him call Tatiana his, because she definitely wasn't. Also, he sounded dumb as hell. Even if Tatiana and I had no involvement, I would still lookout for her because she's his woman. Why wouldn't he want me to? Shit, if I hired some hit men, I would have them muthafuckas looking after everyone I loved and if they didn't, it would be off with their fucking heads for sure.

"Your job is to make sure no one fucks with me; I got Tatiana. She don't need you keeping an eye on her. That's what I'm for; I'm her man, so when you hear us arguing or doing whatever, make sure you just keep it pushing."

I laughed angrily, just as I came to a red light. I felt my phone vibrate, and when I looked down I saw it was a text from Merce. I looked over at him briefly, and then opened my iPhone to view the text message.

Merce: Let it go, there is a bigger picture you have to focus on.

Inhaling, I locked my phone and placed it into the cup holder. Merce was right. I needed to keep my cool and let this nigga think what he needed to. But how could I sit back and watch him and Tatiana argue? And God forbid he tries to put his hands on her. I would kill his ass with no hesitation.

"You right my bad," I finally responded after getting my mind right.

"I know I am," Brevin replied cockily. I simply nodded coolly, trying to ignore his smart-ass mouth, because in a minute I was gonna be putting my .45 in it.

After running Brevin's bitch ass around so he could check on his traps and actually handle business, something he rarely did, the sun had set and it was pretty dark. He wanted to stop home to shower before going to the club, and even though neither Merce or I were in the mood for clubbing, we didn't want to miss out on eavesdropping on some shit that could help us out in the long run. Right now was the play it cool and observe stage, so I wanted to have all the information I needed to pull the rug from under Brevin's hoe ass.

When we got inside of the house, Brevin rushed up the stairs to go shower, but since I smelled food I headed towards the kitchen to see if it was my baby.

"Aye, what you doing?" Merce gripped my shoulder, which I snatched.

"Going to see if Tati is in the kitchen."

"You really think it's a good idea right now?"

"Don't care." I shrugged and walked off.

My ass lit up upon seeing my baby girl at the stove cooking. For a minute I thought it would be their maid Suzanne, but I'm happy I was wrong.

Coming up behind her, I gripped her miniature frame and inhaled the scent of her hair before kissing the back of her head. I loved her ass so fucking much; too fucking much. I hated not being able to sleep with her in my bed at night, but most importantly that we had to pretend we weren't in love.

"Hey," she whispered before turning to face me after she turned the stove off.

"Come get in the shower with me," I leaned down to kiss all over her neck.

"Tef, isn't he here?"

"Yeah but we can shower while he's showering, and be out before he even knows it."

Nibbling on her lip, she looked up at me for a few. I started kissing her lips and groping her body, so she threw her arms around my neck.

"I will meet you," she giggled.

I took off out of the kitchen, through the foyer, and to the bedroom I slept in. I picked out my fit, some clean boxers, and jewelry, then went into the bathroom to turn the shower on. By the time I got down to nothing, Tatiana walked in and pulled her dress over her head. She wasn't wearing anything under but panties, so I immediately closed the bathroom door behind her and started taking them off.

I helped her into the shower after she tied her hair up, and then climbed in after her.

"I love you, Tef," she moaned as I kissed all over her neck.

"I love you more baby."

I trailed my lips down to her nipples and sucked them hungrily before lifting her body up. The water had completely covered her, but she was so small that it was easy for me to hold her tightly. Bringing her down onto my dick, I had to force myself inside, and once in, we both moaned louder than we wanted to. Gripping her ass cheeks, I pressed her into my body more to spread her legs wider, then started gliding her up and down my pole.

"I'm gonna cum already," she whined, holding onto my neck for dear life. Her skin was so soft, and whatever she was wearing for a scent, the water reactivated it because it was permeating the air.

"Tell me you love me again, Tati."

I put her up against the wall and started to beat it up. Her face knotted as soft cries burst through her lips with every thrust. She was so wet and her pussy was pulling me in, making sure I wouldn't be able to pull out.

"I love you so much!" She cried just as she came.

I let her down and then bent her over, away from the showerhead. I didn't want to chance Brevin seeing her hair all wet up and get suspicious.

I slipped back into her as her palms stayed flat against the shower wall. Once I had her tiny waist gripped in my hands, I began pummeling her as she whimpered and cooed. Her ass was small, but still had some jiggle to it along with a sexy smooth texture.

"Shit," I grumbled, biting down on my lip.

The way the water dripped off of me and onto her had my dick swelling. I spanked her ass, just before holding them apart, and the sight of my dick slamming into her wet pussy caused me to nut all inside of her unexpectedly.

Throwing my head back, I panted before sliding out.

I washed both of us off, while kissing her lips every now and again. We stepped out and dried off, and I helped her get dressed before checking outside of my bedroom to see if anyone was around. When the coast was clear, I let her know.

"Remind me that we have to talk okay?" She touched my chest as she started out.

I grabbed her arm and asked, "About what?"

"Later. I don't want to get caught."

I watched her walk off back to the kitchen and wondered how much longer I could do this fake shit.

15

CHAPTER THREE

Merce

I opened my eyes to see Jadynn standing over me holding a tray of food. Rubbing my hands down my face, I sat up and scanned the room, finally remembering that I'd slept over her place last night. Shit, how could I even forget, as deep as I was inside of her until the damn sun started to show its ass.

"What is this for?" I quizzed, sitting up and letting my upper body rest against her headboard.

"I guess to thank you."

"Thank me?" I shoved some of the crispy bacon into my mouth. "For what exactly?"

"For taking up for me with the situation with Russell."

"You're welcome I guess. You don't have to thank me for no shit like that. Like I told you before, any nigga that disrespects you is gonna hear from me. He's lucky I didn't kill his ass."

"Calvin!"

"I'm dead serious. Where I'm from, niggas get killed for shit like what his bitch ass did. Only reason I didn't was because I knew you didn't want me to."

"We're from the same place," she laughed. "Cleveland."

"Yeah but we were raised differently. We both had a two parent home, but the places I stayed and hung out were different from where you did."

"How do you know?" She twisted her face up but I could tell I was right about what I'd said.

"I can just tell."

I finished eating my food, and then took a hot shower in Jadynn's bathroom. Her shower was nice as hell so I took my time, enjoying the hot water and letting it wake me up. I needed to be alert when I went to my crib and checked on my brother. I didn't like allowing him to parlay up in my shit alone, but I had to remind myself it was just for right now. As soon as Teflon and I got rid of Brevin's ass, we could move out of his shit and live in our own.

After brushing my teeth, I got dressed simply in some black sweats, socks, slides, and a wife beater with a white t-shirt over it. After draping my chain around my neck and putting on my cap, Jadynn walked up behind me and hugged my torso. I turned around to look down into her pretty face, and moved her reddish brown hair back.

"You're leaving me?"

"For a little bit, just to handle some business."

"You're lucky I have to be at work or I wouldn't let you go."

"Trust, I don't want to leave but I have to go and see about my little brother and make sure he ain't got a damn house party with cocaine being sniffed everywhere."

"Oh yeah, you told me about him."

"Come through tonight though." I pecked her a couple times, and then she walked me to the door to leave.

I sped from Jadynn's spot to my own in the Quay apartments. I couldn't get out the car fast enough, because I was panicking that he'd ransacked my shit for some reason. I know I sound like I'm being over the top but my little brother was a fuck up and it was obvious he couldn't tell right from wrong, even being as old as he was.

"Bash!" I yelled out as soon as I stepped into my shit.

The smell of weed smoke hit me like a ton of bricks. As my eyes scanned my living room from afar, I saw two pizza boxes and beer bottles sprawled all across the coffee table and on the floor. I could hear the sound of music playing lowly, coming from my spare bedroom, so I darted to the back to go in on this nigga for leaving my living room looking like a pig sty.

"Ah!" Some bitch screamed as she rolled off Sebastian, titties out and everything.

"Nigga when the fuck did I say you could bring these hoes up in my shit!" I roared, snatching that bitch's dress up and tossing it in her face. "Room is funky as fuck and I don't know who to blame for the shit!"

"Man, chill," Sebastian smiled, obviously high as hell.

"Ma, get up out of my crib alive while you still can."

She hopped up quickly after pulling her dress over her head, and then grabbed her underwear from the sectional I had in the room.

"Call me," she had the nerve to say to Sebastian once she reached the threshold of the bedroom door.

"Get out!" I barked, making her jump and scurry off.

I made sure her ass left, and then took my ass right back to the bedroom that Sebastian was laid up in. The nigga had the nerve to be lighting up a blunt and loading Netflix on the TV like he was about to chill all damn day.

"Nah." I snatched the blunt from his lips and ashed it.

"Seriously nigga? What the fuck man? I've been in jail and as soon as I get out you're tripping? Man you're worse than the damn warden."

"You ain't just get out of jail nigga, and I have no problem with you occasionally enjoying yourself, but you need to work for it. You ain't got one reason why you should be laid up with a bitch, smoking and watching Netflix, Bash."

"Aight what, you want me to vacuum or some shit," he laughed lazily before running his hand down his face.

"First wash ya ass, then yeah clean up this damn room, the living room, and if you left any dishes in my fuckin' sink, clean that shit up too." He just looked at me, so I snatched the covers off his ashy ass and yelled, "Now nigga!"

"The fuck man," he mumbled, getting up.

I went into my kitchen and ended up just tidying up my damn

self because I couldn't stand the sight of the dirty ass plates he'd left on the counter. How many plates did two people need to use, especially when I had a stack of paper plates that I purposely left out for his dumb ass.

By the time I was done taking out the trash and shit, Sebastian came strolling from the back dressed.

"Come sit down." I ordered, taking a seat on the couch after drying my hands.

"What's good?" He brushed his hair. Yeah, my little bro was one of them niggas who brushed his fade every 10 minutes, using the brush in his pocket.

"You gon' have to put in some work somewhere legally, or you gon' have to live with mom and dad."

"What? Why? You have money, and extra room, Merce."

"Don't matter. I'm not gonna be taking care of a grown ass man. You're twenty-five Sebastian, you need to be taking care of yo' own shit."

"So what I need to do?"

"Figure the shit out my nigga! Just like I figured shit out for myself, I need you to do the same. I moved out when I was twenty-two, Bash. Not saying you should have too, but I'm trying to show you that you ain't no damn baby and it's time you figure your shit out."

"I hear you. I hear you."

CHAPTER FOUR

Jadynn Davidsen

Two days later…

"So how is everything?" I asked Tatiana as we sat in her kitchen about to eat. Brevin wasn't home, so I felt comfortable enough to ask.

"It's still weird as hell for me, you know, pretending with Brevin and all that jazz. You won't believe how many times Teflon and I have had sex," she whispered the last part while smiling.

"While Brevin was here?" I grinned widely just thinking about it and she nodded. "I bet that was scary as hell. I'm surprised you could get going."

"It actually made it better. The thrill of possibly getting caught intensified the sex for me. I know I sound crazy but it's true."

"It does but I can kind of see how that would make things better." We laughed in unison.

"But enough about me, my situation has been the same for

months you know that. Are you still getting it good from Merce," she beamed.

I didn't respond for a minute because I wanted to just admire my best friend's happiness. For the last couple of years she'd been so depressed and just going through life, not really living. Even though her situation was hella complicated right now, she was so much happier and you could see it in the way she walked and talked.

"What?" She finally questioned me since I was sitting there simply smiling.

"Nothing I just like seeing you like this. I admit I didn't know what to expect between you and Teflon, but I'm loving him right now. Even if you guys don't last, I still appreciate him coming in and making you feel good for a little while."

"Yeah me too. I was worried about him being the same old thing, because I do remember a time where Brevin was the sweetest guy on earth."

"Too long ago because I barely remember," I half joked.

It was vague, but I sort of remembered a time where Brevin was an okay dude. It was in the very beginning when he was trying to win her over; the time when most niggas hide how whack and trifling they are.

"Stop trying to shift the conversation from you to me, Jadynn."

"Yeah Calvin and I are good."

"Ooh Calvin? I forgot his real name, but you two must be close if you're calling him by his government name."

"Can't help it. But that means nothing because you still call Teflon… Teflon."

"That's because his name is strange as hell. I have to get used to it before I start calling him that on the regular."

"You're ridiculous," I chuckled. "But honestly I have no idea what Calvin and I are. We just kind of went from talking to one another on some friend shit, to going on a date and sleeping together. We spend the night together a few times out of the week and talk on the phone or text when we don't. I don't know, but I don't want to assume."

"Please don't assume. You'll walk up on him kissing another woman doing that. And niggas love saying, 'We ain't exclusive. I never said we were,'" she mocked a male voice as we chuckled together.

"Trust me I know."

After chatting with Tatiana for a little longer, we went to the nail shop and then parted ways. My conversation with her had me thinking about what Merce and I were. I didn't want to ask because truthfully, we'd just met and I didn't want him thinking I was some crazy bitch who expected a wedding after three months of knowing one another. But on the flip side, I wasn't too comfortable with sleeping with him without a title.

I don't know about other women, but I couldn't deal with a man that I knew was sleeping with other girls. You don't know what his other bitch is doing, and that's how you catch shit. In addition to me not wanting to be some fuck buddy on the side, I felt like he and I were getting close emotionally too. If anything all this shit crumbling would hurt worse if my feelings were completely involved. So yeah, I've made up my mind. I'm gonna come right out and ask his ass what's going on, but somehow make it sound like I'm not pressuring him to grow old with me.

***

That night…

"How is everything going with Sebastian?" I questioned, lying on Merce's chiseled chest. I know, I should have talked to him before letting him fuck me, but just in case our conversation turned into an argument and ended things, I wanted to get one last dick down in.

"I don't fucking know. He claims he's gonna get his shit together but we'll see. Nigga is old as fuck, still trying to get breastfed."

I laughed.

"I think he just needs time to adjust. You and you're parents have been babying him in a sense all his life. He needs to gradually stand on his own two feet."

"I don't know what the fuck he needs, but gradually or not, he's got one month to figure that shit out."

"So mean," I giggled, enjoying the feel of his abs under my hands. "So we're cool right?" I picked my head up and laid it on the pillow so I could look into his eyes.

"Well shit I hope so. With the way I just made you cum, we better be cool."

"No." I sat up, covering my body with the sheet. He simply yanked it down, exposing me. "I meant like are we boyfriend and girlfriend? Or is this like a friends with benefits."

"You tell me."

"I can't just choose, Calvin. We have to come to an agreement on something like this. Do you umm, want me to be your girlfriend?"

He stared up at me for a while, teeth sunken into his bottom lip. He was so sexy in a rough kind of way. My taste in men had changed since being with him. I no longer wanted the clean-cut niggas.

"I do, but I want it to be like this. How it is already. It seems like once you start putting titles on shit, muthafuckas act differently."

"Muthafuckas meaning women?"

He shrugged.

"I mean yeah. Whenever y'all get close to making shit official, it's like a switch goes off in y'all mind, saying to start acting like some controlling ass psycho."

I laughed and shook my head, lying back down on my side. He turned on his and pecked me, before moving my hair from my face.

"Guys change too. I think a switch goes off in their heads saying to turn into an incompetent asshole, who can't keep his dick in his pants."

"Aight then so how about we agree to not let that switch turn on."

"Okay." I nodded. "But I'm letting you know now, if you sleep with any of my family members, I'm throwing hot grits on your ass."

Laughing, exposing his beautiful smile, he shook his head.

"So you telling me I don' had my eye on your mama this whole time and I can't hit?" We both chortled loudly as I hit him in the chest. "I would never do no shit like that though. I can't see myself cheating at all, but if I did, which I won't so calm down with the facial expressions… it wouldn't be with anybody you loved."

"Thank you."

He yanked me closer to him and kissed me hungrily, before positioning himself on top of me. Placing my legs onto his shoulders, he entered me slowly, filling me up so that I had to whimper. He stared down into my eyes as he moved in and out of me, getting me wetter every time I hit the base of him. I swear I felt like his dick was about to come through my mouth. It felt so good that I had to fight the urge to tell him I loved him, so I just bit down on my lip, and pressed the back of my head into the pillow.

CHAPTER FIVE

Tatiana

Teflon, Merce, and I were sitting at the table eating the big French toast breakfast that Suzanne made. Brevin came home drunk last night, so he wouldn't be up until around 3pm. Before Teflon, that shit used to bother me, and I would attempt to wake him around noon. But these days, I loved when Brevin would sleep his day away. I didn't have to worry about him breathing down my neck for sex, and I could spend time with Teflon.

"I have to go pick my brother up so I can take him to his interview, but Teflon when I get back we have some shit to discuss aight?" Merce rose to his feet and picked his plate up.

"Yeah. Meet me at the park though," Teflon spoke lowly.

"Aight."

Once Merce left the kitchen, Teflon and I shared a smile as we continued to eat. I was trying to think of a good time to tell him I was pregnant. I knew when he found out, he would go overboard with trying to protect me, which may fuck his plan up.

"You okay?" He quizzed, gulping down his orange juice.

"Yeah I'm fine I just want to talk to you when you get some time okay?"

"I have time now. I'm gon' always make time for you, no matter what." I loved how he could turn off his street demeanor for me. Teflon was the sweetest guy I'd ever met, and I just prayed he never changed.

"I know baby, but I have to go to a meeting. Eddie got a new client, a restaurant owner, and he hired us to help with his opening."

"Nice, so what are you gonna do?"

"Just basically find out what his angle is, and then I'm gonna meet with Angie, this journalist I know and see if she can come to the grand opening and also write up on the restaurant. Then Jadynn and I will split the work between contacting other media," I sighed, standing up and collecting our plates.

After dropping them into the sink, I walked to Teflon and leaned down to kiss him. His already slanted eyes were low, and his teeth were digging into his bottom lip. I chuckled as he brought me down into his lap, because I already knew what he had in mind.

"Where you going without giving me my kiss?" He groaned before pecking me and then sucking my lips. His big hand groped my thigh, his favorite feature of mine.

We sat there kissing for a little while, pressing our faces together. I caressed the side of his face as our tongues entangled, and just thought about how I couldn't wait for us to be able to do this for as long as we wanted and when we wanted.

"Oh shit!" I shot up from Teflon's lap when I saw Suzanne dart from the kitchen.

"What, Tati?"

"Nothing, I have to go."

Shit!

I grabbed my purse and then rushed out of the house. I wanted to go after Suzanne, but I didn't have time for that right now. This restaurant guy was a big deal, and Eddie would murder me in cold blood if I did anything to mess this opportunity up. Once I was inside of my car, I cranked up and peeled out, putting my seatbelt on, on the way.

I stood outside of Zeus' apartment door, preparing a few questions in my head. He stayed in a nice building downtown on Saint Clair Avenue, and I expected something nice since he was clearly made of money if he'd hired Eddie's firm.

I knocked lightly on the door, and then waited patiently. A woman wearing a black silk robe answered the door, and she tightened it when she saw me.

"Can I help you?"

"Oh uh," I glanced at the door number to make sure I was at the right one. "Yeah, is Mr. Zeus Rydell in?"

"What did you need with Zeus?"

Jealous girlfriend I see. I wasn't gonna give her a hard time though because I could be the same with Teflon. I didn't like women looking at him, talking to him, or doing anything with him. I was never this possessive over Brevin, at least nothing out of the norm. But when it came to Tre'Wayne German, I didn't play.

"I'm Tatiana Drew, and I'm with Penrose PR. I need to discuss a few things with Mr. Rydell about his upcoming grand opening."

"Circe who is—" Zeus came to the door and stopped talking upon seeing me. "Hi, you must be Tatiana Drew."

"Yeah I am."

"Come in." He stepped back smiling, holding the door open for me.

I expected him to be much older than he was, or at least older than he looked. He was tall, light skinned, with a low cut fade, and trimmed facial hair. He was in shape, which I knew because he was standing in front of me in his pajama pants and no shirt.

"Umm, please make yourself comfortable and give me a few moments. I hope you're in no rush, I totally forgot about this meeting with all that's going on."

"Nope, not in a rush."

"Okay be right back. Have a seat uh… anywhere."

I nodded with my brows raised as he closed the front door and jogged to the back. I decided to take a seat in his living room because his couch looked more comfortable than his chairs. I wasn't showing one bit, but I was already feeling tired throughout the day and didn't want to be uncomfortable while here. Sitting down on the brown leather couch, I started to remove my legal pad from my bag, along with a pen.

"So what do you do?" Circe, his lady friend quizzed me. I'd totally forgotten that she was even here in the living area.

"I do public relations. I basically help people, businesses, and venues build a great reputation through media, newspaper, and word of mouth."

"Circe, offer her something to drink!" Zeus yelled from the back before slamming some door from the back of the apartment.

Circe raised her eyebrow at me, which I guess was her way of asking, but I just shook my head no and put my hand up.

"So did you *choose* to work with Zeus?" She pulled a chair out and sat at the table, which was pretty close to the couch.

"Choose him?"

"Yeah was it your idea to work with him?"

"Actually I believe Mr. Rydell contacted my boss Eddie, looking for representation. I don't choose clients, I simply work with them once my boss has brought them on."

"Right," she fake smiled and tossed her dark hair from one side to the other. She looked like a Victoria's Secret model. She was tall compared to me, with deep chocolate skin, a gap in her two front teeth, and doe eyes. She was extremely beautiful, but clearly insecure. "Well just in case he gets friendly with you, I want you to know that he's taken and we're soon to be engaged."

Chuckling, I shook my head and wrote down a few things on my legal pad.

"Something funny?" She raised a brow.

"I uh, have just never heard of anyone being soon to be engaged. But you have nothing to worry about. I'm very happy in my relationship, thank you."

"Well—"

"Circe can you give us some privacy." Zeus returned wearing a white short sleeved button up, with gray slacks and expensive looking shoes. He smelled really good, and looked almost as good too. He scratched his low cut beard as he checked the time on his big white-gold watch, before sitting down across from me and smiling. I couldn't help but to smile back.

"Just act like I'm not here babe."

"I told you to give us some privacy. Matter fact, go to the store and pick up the things I wrote down on that Post-It on the front of the fridge."

Circe stared at his side profile for a little bit, and then shot up out the chair to storm into his kitchen.

"Excuse me, beautiful."

He got up to follow her, and I could hear him saying something to her but I couldn't make out what. Pushing my hair behind my ears, I pretended to look out the window of the apartment as Circe walked back by and left out.

"I hope I didn't cause you to lose a girlfriend," I joked when Zeus returned.

"No, not at all. But I'm sure you have caused a few problems for other men."

He watched me lustfully as I crossed my legs. I was wearing a black halter dress with a black blazer on top. The dress wasn't too short, but it did show a little thigh. My shoes were sandal stilettos in black. My curly hair brushed the top of my shoulders as I reached in my bag to get some book tab Post-Its.

"Actually no. At least not that I know of."

"The prettiest ones are always oblivious to just how beautiful they are."

I chuckled lowly before straightening up and clearing my throat.

"Thank you, Mr. Rydell. Now—"

"Zeus, please call me Zeus. Can I call you Tatiana?"

"Yes that's fine. Now what exactly is the message you want to convey with your restaurant and with your opening? For example, is it a sophisticated and sexy dining spot, or is it more chic and fun, for a younger crowd?"

"Definitely sophisticated and sexy. That's more my style. I take it that, that's your style as well, Tatiana?"

"Oh I like a little bit of everything. But okay great." I started writing down some ideas under my sophisticated and sexy column. "What do you think about a gold, white, and black theme?"

"I uh, I love it."

"Good."

We continued discussing details with him throwing out compliments every now and again. I wanted to remain professional, so I didn't shut him down like I usually would have. Plus, he was being harmless, and his flirting wasn't going to get him anything anyway.

"Alright well I think we have everything down. I'm gonna get with my colleague, Jadynn Davidsen, and we'll make a list of some outlets to contact. I will meet you with again after that for an update." I stood up and put my things away, and then handed him my business card.

"Can we meet over dinner? My treat."

"How about a business lunch, your treat?"

He chuckled and nodded before saying, "Works for me. But then once the business is out the way, can we have a get to know you dinner?"

"I'm flattered Mr. Rydell, but I'd like to keep things professional." He didn't need to know about Teflon. And I wasn't gonna mention my baby because for one, I was only an hour and a half pregnant, and on top of that I had had bad luck with babies and I didn't want to jinx this one; specially because it was the baby I'd made with Teflon. That's not to say I didn't love the ones I'd made with Brevin.

"Oh sorry, of course."

"And it looks like you're in a relationship." I put my bag over my shoulder. "I will be in touch to set up a meeting time after I get with Jadynn. Have a good day, Mr. Rydell." I started towards the door and he opened it for me.

"Please, Tatiana, call me Zeus."

"It was a pleasure, Mr. Rydell."

He needed to know we would not be getting familiar enough to be on first name basis.

CHAPTER SIX

Teflon

Later that evening…

Brevin sent Merce and I on an errand to check on his traps. He wanted us to be sure that no one was hanging around them and looking suspicious. When I say I was dead tired of this nigga, I meant the shit. Every time he asked me to do something, I had to tell myself not to blow his damn brains out. Merce and I were here to have his back as far as making sure that none of his enemies got close to him. Running around like some damn errand boys wasn't a part of the job description.

I would have gladly told his ass that, but Merce and I needed a reason to get out the house for a little bit, and together. If we just tried to leave, Brevin would want to join, and we'd end up at some strip club watching him basically beg for pussy.

"Sorry, Cecily was tripping about me not spending enough time with the family when I tried to leave," Groove walked up and sat down at the park bench that Merce and I were at. "Had to calm her ass down so when I got back home tonight she wouldn't be holding out."

"It's cool," Merce nodded as I chuckled.

Groove and Cecily had been together for a while, and they'd always been attached at the hip. He'd dabbled a little with other women, but it was never anything serious.

I was sure Cecily didn't like the fact that Groove worked so much because that meant they had to be apart a lot.

"I'm thinking we should do the obvious. Let's hit his traps, and then play the 'I got your back' card. He'll think that we're out here trying to help, but the whole time we'll be taking his shit down, along with his allies," I whispered even though the park was a dead zone at the moment.

"I can fuck with that, but my only thing is, if we destroy everything, how long is it gonna take for us to build the shit back up," Merce frowned.

"We need to work simultaneously," Groove chimed in and I nodded because that's what I was about to say.

"Exactly. While we're cleaning the house out, we need to be shopping for new shit to put in it. All three of us don't have to be on one task at a time." I glanced around the park, before landing my eyes back on Merce and Groove. "The main goal here is to pump fear in his people's hearts, kill off the ones who got his back, and then eventually get at him, that Carnie spy nigga, and Mack."

"I think Mack can help us betray that nigga Brevin. Then once we get Brevin out the way, we can off his ass too," Groove nodded.

"How you figure? This nigga rides for Brevin knowing that Brevin is fucking his bitch. I don't see him turning on that nigga anytime soon, Groove," Merce shook his head.

"He will. Nigga low-key hates that nigga and it's because of Gloria. Only reason he ain't done shit is because he's too damn scared and he know he ain't got the ammo to really go at Brevin. We have to make that nigga think we on his team, get him to feel like we got his back and Brevin doesn't."

I smiled as I listened to Groove. Shit anything that was gonna get Brevin out the way I was with. I just wanted to speed this shit up because I was tired of hiding my damn relationship with my girl. I was even more tired of seeing that nigga all in her face. I swear, if I didn't think that he'd do something to Tatiana once he found out about us, I'd say fuck him. This shit was all for her. Getting his bread and empire was just a bonus, but he could legit keep all that shit if he'd let me take her unscathed. But he wouldn't so he had to go. And because I had to get rid of Brevin, I had to get rid of his army too.

Merce, Groove, and I chatted for a little bit longer, and then Merce and I headed back to Brevin's crib.

"Aye I want to get shit popping ASAP," I told Merce as we stood in my room.

"I know. Shit me too. So let's stop talking and get to work."

I nodded, not wanting to say too much in this nigga's house. I was already pushing it by fucking Tatiana in here, but that was some shit I couldn't help.

Everything about her was addictive as hell. I hated to sound like some soft ass muthafucka, but Tatiana had me right where most bitches wanted their nigga. And I never thought any woman would have me legit willing to die for them that wasn't my mother. If anything I assumed it'd be Kayla.

I hopped into the shower once Merce left my bedroom, and shook my head. I wanted to be back in my own spot so damn bad. After cleaning up, I brushed, flossed, rinsed, and then hopped into the big ass bed. This was the best part of my fucking day for sure.

I hadn't been sleep for long, when I felt someone getting into my bed. It was dark as hell in the room, but I already knew who it was. I turned to face Tatiana, and pushed her thick brown curly hair from her face.

"Baby, what I tell you about coming down here?" I laughed as she nuzzled her miniature frame into mine. She was so small, and I was big as fuck, but we were a perfect fucking match in my book.

"I couldn't sleep. It's so hard sleeping next to him and not you."

Exhaling heavily, I caressed her smooth back as my mind raced a mile a minute.

"Just one more month, Tati, if that. I promise I'm gonna be on this shit, and once he's gone we can do the normal shit like sleep in the bed together." I tilted her head back and pressed my lips against hers.

"Tef," she whispered against my lips.

I put my hand between her legs to spread them, as I pushed her onto her back. Gripping the waist of her underwear, I started to pull them down her sexy ass legs.

"Teflon I'm pregnant."

Stopping in my tracks, I let her underwear fall from my hands as I stared down into her face. Her full lips were parted as she waited for my response.

"With my baby?"

"Yes who else?" she hit my abs and frowned.

"Nah I know umm, I was just making sure." I looked off and then back down at her. "So that means you'll marry me once this shit is all over?"

"Get married?"

"Yeah married. You know, when two muthafuckas fall in love and make shit legal. You love a nigga right?"

"Of course."

"Then that'll be the plan."

"I just, I want to be sure that you want to get married for real. We haven't even been together a year, so you don't have to if you don't want to."

"I know that, and I also know how long we've been together. I told you how I feel about you and how different shit is between us, Tati. I love you way more than that bitch upstairs, and you were gonna marry his ass."

"Okay," she giggled and tugged on my wrist. I pushed my boxers down and then off, before lying down between her legs. Pushing her gown down her shoulders, I flicked my tongue over her nipples as she moaned softly.

I crushed my lips against hers as I forced my way inside of her, and we both just froze at the feeling, before we resumed tonguing one another down.

"You are so damn sexy to me." I yanked the covers up over us, and continued to make love to her.

***

The next morning…

I opened my eyes and immediately looked next to me to see that Tatiana was gone. I could still smell that sweet scent of lotion she put on after her nighttime baths, so I buried my face into the pillow for a little bit to savor it. She had me sick. And I think part of this was all because I couldn't have her all day and proudly like I wanted to.

My phone started to ring, and when I saw it was all the way over on my damn dresser I groaned. Climbing out the bed, I grabbed my boxers from the floor before slipping them on. When I picked up my phone, I sighed because I already knew who the fuck it was.

As soon as I answered, a female voice said, "This call may be recorded. I have a call from Torrey, an inmate at Lorain Correctional Institute. Do you accept the charges?"

Running my hand down my face I replied, "Yes."

"Damn, sound like you ain't know if you were gonna accept the shit little bro," Torrey laughed.

"What's up, T? How you holding up?"

"I'm aight, well was aight. I'm better now because I'll be home in a month."

"For real?" I sat down on the bed. I didn't want my brother locked up, but I knew all he did was fuck shit up when he was out.

"Yeah man, just found out yesterday. So you got shit set up for me when I get out right? And you making sure Audrina is keeping her legs closed?"

"Nigga I got my own shit to worry about! I don't work for you! All I can say is that you won't be struggling when you step out. I may drop by Audrina's tomorrow, but she ain't doing shit with another nigga you know that. I gave mama money to give to her and TJ."

"Thanks. So yeah, one damn month from today, be down here in Grafton to get me."

"I'll think about it." I hung up.

I hated that, that nigga always thought he ran shit because he was the oldest. He was sadly mistaken. And if he thought he was about to come out here and just be on through me, he would again have me fucked up.

CHAPTER SEVEN

Brevin Williamson

Two days later...

$\mathscr{I}$ woke up feeling terrible as fuck. I didn't do shit yesterday but drink, and have Suzanne cook me meals all day. I knew I was supposed to have a couple meetings, but I called them off, then had Teflon and Merce go check my traps. I usually would have Mack handle the meetings, but I think that nigga was starting to feel himself a little too much and I wasn't with that shit. Cleveland was my muthafucking city, and I would remind any nigga who needed reminding.

Looking over to Tatiana's side of the bed, I saw it was made up. I missed her ass like crazy, and even though she swore we were good, I felt a disconnection. We didn't sleep together because she was always working, busy around the house, or too tired. And me, shit I was always twisted so I slept a lot. But I would make sure we ended that drought. Tatiana had that pussy that would fuck yo' head up, so I needed a hit like a crack head needed crack.

Snatching up my ringing phone, I groaned when I saw it was 2pm, and Groove was calling. Nigga stayed on me about handling my business, and I hated the shit. However, I knew he was just doing it to have my back.

"What's popping?" I chuckled, massaging my aching head.

"Nigga why you sound like you just woke up?"

"Because I just fucking woke up my nigga. What you need?"

"I need you to be on your shit. It's 2pm in the damn afternoon and you're just now waking up, Brevin. You been drinking?"

"Nah," I chuckled and heard him suck his teeth. "Aye, I'm young and I'm rich, I can drink and do whatever the fuck I want."

"Well you won't be rich for long if you don't get back on yo' shit my nigga. Two of your traps got vandalized and robbed."

"What?" I sat up, throwing the covers off. "Fuck umm, call Teflon and Merce. Have them take a look at the shit and talk to people."

"And what you gon' do?"

"Uh, shit. Once y'all are done, I'm want to meet at the house aight? Fuck! I wonder if Tef and Merce are already here. Look just call them anyways because I ain't got time to run downstairs and say shit."

"Aight but—"

"Just handle it for now and we'll meet when them niggas are done." I hung up the phone and then went into the bathroom to brush my teeth. When I finished, my phone starting ringing again, and I saw it was Amanda."

"I told you get the fuck out my life didn't I?" I answered, leaving it on speakerphone.

Shit, Tatiana knew everything now so if she were here, which I knew she wasn't, it wouldn't be anything new. I'd try to keep my lie up, but two nights ago Tatiana forced me to admit that Amanda's baby could possibly be mine. She was cooler about it than I thought. Guess I had it like that.

"Brev I'm sorry! I only told Tatiana because—"

"This ain't even about you telling her shit!" I picked up and roared into the phone. "This is about the fucking fact that I told you to abort that muthafucka!"

"This is your child! You can't talk like that about it!"

"I say what I want! If you think I'm about to help you out and play family, then you got shit twisted. Only kids I'm claiming, are the ones coming from my damn fiancée!"

"Brevin," she cried. I just sat there on the phone, listening to her stupid ass sob. I tried to save her from feeling like this, which is why I'd said to get rid of it. I didn't care if the child was mine, which I couldn't be too sure about; I was not taking care of it.

"Look I gotta go, ma. Peace."

I hopped into the shower, and once I was clean to my liking, I made my way to the kitchen where I found Suzanne. She was wiping the stove off, and when she saw me she smiled awkwardly.

"Good morning… well I guess afternoon. You plan on making lunch anytime soon?" I sat at the bar. I had some time to kill before Teflon and Merce came back to me with some details.

"I was just about to get that started. What did you have a taste for, Mr. Williamson."

"That Lemon chicken shit you make, along with some rice."

"Of course. I may need about an hour. Would you like a smoothie while you wait for me to finish?"

"That's cool." I sat back and went into my phone to text message Tatiana. I felt like I didn't even have a damn fiancée and that needed to change.

Me: I miss us. What time will you be home today?

Tati: Not sure. I have a big project, but hopefully before 7pm.

Me: Aight I will be here. I wanna be up in that tonight. I miss it.

I waited for a response, but she never sent one. I just shrugged it off, telling myself that maybe she'd gotten busy. If I had to pin her ass down tonight I would.

"Here is your smoothie." Suzanne placed the tall glass filled with a light purple substance on the bar, and then put a straw in it.

"Thanks. Let me ask you something. Do Tatiana and I seem the same?"

Her facial expression changed from happy to worrisome in a quick ass second. I was scared as hell, wondering what she was about to say.

"What do you mean?"

"Like does our relationship appear to have changed? A part of me feels like we've drifted a bit since that whole baby situation."

"Oh, well, yeah I believe that this time really bothered her since she was so far along. But I think you should maybe do something nice for her, and show her that you care."

"Hmm, I guess."

I finished off my smoothie, held conversations with a couple bird hoes that couldn't take a hint, and by that time, my lunch was ready. Not once did Tatiana reply to my text message. As soon as I finished, Groove, Merce, and Teflon walked through the door.

"Oh, uh follow me." I led them to the den, and once everyone was seated, I had Suzanne make us all a drink. "I think she likes you, Tef," I chuckled, sipping my bourbon.

"Who?" He frowned.

"Suzanne. I mean she's a little older, but I'm sure everything still works for her." I chuckled to myself as I thought about it. Suzanne was staring hard at Teflon.

"Can we get to business," Groove scoffed. Nigga was always too damn serious.

"Yeah so what they say about my shit being fucked up?" I questioned, eyes darting from Merce to Teflon and vice versa.

"They ain't say shit because there was no one left at that trap that could talk," Merce replied.

"The fuck? They killed all my niggas working that house?"

"Yep." Teflon stared me in the eyes with a blank expression.

I still didn't too much care for his ass after we fought, but he and Merce were about the only two niggas out here that I felt comfortable enough with having my back. Niggas hated me out here, so not too many muthafuckas wanted to protect me. It was like a sure thing that you'd get popped if you did.

"Fuck. Aight look, Groove I need you to move some of my guys from another house to that one—"

"It's been burned to the ground," Teflon said.

"Fuck!" Shaking my head and sighing I said, "Well Groove find another spot for me to get and then move some niggas from that spot to the new one. Merce I need you to watch houses when you're not with me, and Teflon you do the same when you're not with me. If I don't leave the house, go together. I don't need y'all getting shot. As soon as y'all see any damn thing, hit my line to inform me, and then take care of it."

"And what you gon' do?" Merce questioned. I kind of felt like he was trying to imply that I wasn't doing shit, but now wasn't the time for me to get in his ass.

"I'm gonna be handling business, making sure that the product is still being delivered, and business deals are going through."

"One of us will be there right? To make sure you're good?" Teflon quizzed.

"Exactly, while the other party is keeping a watchful eye."

"Cool," Groove nodded and patted my back.

The four of us sat there drinking and talking until it was dark outside, and by then I heard the front door slam. I knew it was Tatiana, so I rose to my feet, ready to leave. When I looked at the clock, I shook my head seeing it was 8:30pm.

"Aye umm, what about your girl? We're protecting you, but who's protecting her? She's the first thing niggas will attack to get to you." Merce let me know.

"Groove, you look after her when you have time."

I couldn't sacrifice Teflon and Merce not watching over me just so that they could watch Tatiana. I know it sounded shady as fuck, but I disagreed with Merce. I didn't think a nigga would fuck with Tatiana. One had yet to, and since I hadn't been smashing any other nigga's bitches for the past two weeks, I wasn't worried. The beef I had right now was simply over territory… at least that's what it seemed like.

I made my way out of the den and went up to the bedroom. When I got there, the bathroom door was closed, so I knew Tatiana was taking one of her many baths. I moved closer to the door, and even though the bathwater running was loud, I could have sworn I heard her throwing up. I kept thinking about that pregnancy test, but the thought of any other nigga getting inside of Tatiana made me feel like I was about to go insane.

"Baby, you okay?" I tried to enter but it was locked.

"Uh, yeah honey I'm fine! Why?"

I heard the toilet flush and the sink come on.

"Are you throwing up?"

"Yeah Eddie had a caterer come to work for breakfast, and I think I ate something bad this morning!" she called from behind the door.

"Aight, I'll be out here waiting for you. I can give you a massage like you like."

I heard nothing in response, and then her turn the water off. I went to sit on the bed after taking out one of her favorite oils that smelled like vanilla and fruit, or some shit along those lines. I changed into some boxers, sweats, and socks, then sat down on the bed to check my text messages. Finally the door opened, and Tatiana came out, already in her nightgown and smelling good as fuck.

"Ready for a rub down?" I grinned, eyeing her body. She didn't have much like I usually preferred, but her pussy trumped it all.

"I was gonna go eat dinner. Did Suzanne finish?"

"Not yet. Come here." I pulled her into my lap and she tensed up a little bit.

I guess she still wasn't over me beating our kid out of her. Shit still fucked with me too, but I was determined to make her feel better and get another baby percolating inside of her soon.

"What did—"

"You know I love you so much right?" I kissed her arm.

"Yeah of course."

"And I'm sorry about all the shit I've done, hitting you, and then Amanda, all that shit. But I've changed and I want you to know I care."

"Okay," she nodded.

Pushing her hair from her face, I kissed her lips softly. She was so stiff, almost like she felt she shouldn't have been doing what we were doing; like she belonged to some other nigga and not me.

"I want to get married, like soon. Let's just get eloped in the next couple of days." I was trying to hold off on our marriage for a little longer, but I felt like she was slipping through my fingers so I had to act fast now.

"Brevin I'd like to have a real wedding."

"And we can baby. But let's make shit official, just you and me, then we can throw a wedding party."

"I—"

"Tatiana what's the problem? We're in love and already engaged. You love me right?"

She looked into my eyes for longer than I wanted her to, before saying, "Ye-yeah of course I do I jus—"

"Then let's do it. I'm thinking this Saturday. I can have Teflon or Merce as a witness for us."

"Yeah sure, okay."

"Cool. You good?"

"I'm perfect Brevin I'd just like to go eat." She moved from my lap and went over to her mirror to pull her thick, shoulder length, curly hair into a ball thing on her head.

I came up behind her and hugged her body into mine. I hated feeling like this. It was like all this time that I'd had her, I didn't really appreciate it. And now that deep down, I could feel our distance, I was panicking. But if she thought she could leave me alive, she had another thing coming.

CHAPTER EIGHT

Merce

$\mathcal{I}$ was sitting outside of the trap on E 66th Street in Hough, while Groove and these two dudes he recruited robbed the trap on Decker Avenue. I lit the tip of the blunt, because as soon as they were done, Groove was gonna meet me over here so we could plan how we were gonna explain the news to Brevin. He had about four more trap houses that we needed to fuck over, and once that was done, we would realize that the blame had been on some of his closest allies. We'd already taken care of that Wade nigga that was starting to take over, so Brevin wouldn't be able to blame him. So after murking Brevin's 'backstabbing allies', we'd dead Brevin, and then Mack.

I ashed the blunt once my phone lit up, and then looked at the text message to see it was from Groove.

G: On our way.

Me: Aight.

I waited for a little bit, and when I saw Groove's car drive by me, I followed him and made a right on Whitney Avenue. We both came to a stop in front of the house, and when we did I hit Brevin to let him know I was going to the trap on Decker Avenue since it was the last one of the night. In a little bit, I would let him know it'd been fucked over as well.

"You hit him?" Groove asked me, as we both neared one another. Some dude was following behind him wearing all black like the both of us.

"Yeah I did. Who you?" I looked to the guy.

"Chauncey but just call me Chance."

"Merce," I replied and he nodded. I looked to Groove who laughed lowly, removing the safety off of his gun.

"He's cool peoples I swear."

"Better be. If not I'm killing both of you niggas." I dropped the blunt I'd been smoking and put it out with my shoe. "Let's go."

The three of us ran back towards 66th street, and made a left, coming up to the house. Once our ski masks were down, we ran up to the front. I beat on the door as hard as I could, and when I saw a dude peer through the rectangle window at the top, while unlocking the door, I blew his head open.

"Oh fuck!" another dude hollered as Groove, Chance, and I came barging in, stepping over the nigga who'd unlocked the door like a dumb ass.

POP! POP!

Groove shot the other nigga in the head as I went to the back to check the other rooms. I found a dude fucking some bitch, so I iced them both before checking the other room. Coming into the kitchen, I spotted Groove and Chance busting out the windows and fucking shit up, so I went to hunt for matches in the kitchen.

I found some in a drawer by the stove, so I struck it and tossed it on the carpet into the living room. Once the flame started to spread, the three of us dipped out, running until we made it back to Whitney where we'd hit a right.

"Get in any fucking car!" I yelled to Chance who was slowing around. He hopped in with me since my whip was the closest, and then we sped down Whitney, making a right on Giddings, headed back to Decker.

Once we made it to that trap, Groove text me to let me know he was calling Brevin to tell him this trap had been robbed, at the same time I was gonna text it to him. Once we both confirmed that he was upset and believed that we'd just found this out, Chance went to get in the car with Groove and I went to my actual home to shower and change clothes. After that, I headed back home to Brevin's crib. When I got there, I went straight to Teflon's room.

"What he say?" he whispered as soon as I closed the door behind myself.

"Same shit, that we need to find out who did it."

"Just two more and then we can put our focus elsewhere. I'll figure out 'who did the shit' and we can let him know after tomorrow."

"Aight fasho."

I dapped him up, then went to get my shit so I could go spend the night with Jadynn. I didn't feel like having a conversation with Brevin tonight, and I missed my girl.

***

The next day...

I was inside of Herb'n Twine off Lorain Avenue, waiting in line to get some sandwiches for Jadynn and I. I felt someone bump into me, and when I looked over my shoulder I saw Savannah smiling. I hadn't talked to her ass in a cool minute, mainly because I was busy trying to fuck over Brevin and then spend time with Jadynn.

"Oh what's up?" I asked dryly, turning back around to face the nigga who worked here.

"You tell me, Merce. I haven't talked to you in a long ass time. I almost thought you moved back to California."

"Nah I didn't."

"So." She hopped in front of me in the line. Hugging my torso, she moved in closer and said, "Can you come over tonight? I can make an enchilada pie for you."

"Aye." I removed her hands from my body and she frowned. "I'm umm, I got a girl and she wouldn't be too fond of me coming through yo' spot, Sav."

"A girl?" She jerked her neck back and folded her arms across her breasts.

"Yeah a girl. And—"

"Wait, hold the fuck up!" she threw her hand up. "I've been on you to grow the hell up and become a man for the longest, yet you decide to grow balls for another hoe? Oh nah, nigga, you got me fucked up!"

"Savannah, calm yo' ass down," I gritted, slightly scanning the establishment because her ass was loud as hell.

"No!"

Gripping her arm, I dragged her ass outside and then hemmed her up against the wall around the corner. It was an alleyway with a gang of graffiti, rocks, and dirt.

"Look, causing a scene ain't gon' do shit for you but get yo' ass knocked the fuck out, Savannah!"

"It's not fair, Calvin! I love you and I thought you loved me! How can you just be with another girl! Who is she?"

"You're stupider than I thought if you think I'm gonna tell you her damn name," I chuckled, squinting my eyes at the sun.

"You need to just come over if you want me to stay off your back. If you don't, I'm gonna make you and that bitch's life a living hell!"

"What the fuck for?" I barked. "You can have any nigga you want!"

"And I want you! I've put in too much damn work to just let you go like that. I even waited for you while you were away in California."

"So no other nigga hit while I was away?"

"Nope. I let their asses know that it wasn't going down like that."

"Aight Savannah. I'm gon' say this shit once, don't fuck with me or my girl, and keep your damn distance. I don't wanna be with yo' ass, and there is nothing you can do to change that. If you try to, shit may not end well for you ma."

"We'll just have to see about that, because like I said, I put years into this that we have, and I didn't do it to give you away to some other bitch." She started off and when I grabbed her arm she snatched it from me.

I really didn't want to kill Savannah because she was a woman for one, and secondly we had too much history. No matter what she did, killing her would fuck with me for the longest. I knew whatever she had planned would be some petty stupid shit, not worth me murking her for. And right now the only thing I could do was let Jadynn know so she'd be prepared. Maybe a well-whooped ass via Jadynn would calm Savannah down.

CHAPTER NINE

Jadynn

I sat behind my desk in my office, just pondering for a little bit. Eddie's floor in the building downtown had cubicles in the middle, and glass offices around the side. Tatiana and I were lucky enough to score offices, but I just wished it wasn't see-through.

At the moment I didn't feel like myself, even though I should have been pretty happy. I had a great boyfriend, a great job, and my health, but for some reason I still found myself feeling down or upset when I got alone or began thinking too hard. It was almost like I was disgusted with myself.

"Busy?" Tatiana peeked her head into my office. She came all the way in, and then closed the wooden door. The office may have been see-through, but it was soundproof which was a plus.

"Actually I've just finished up." I powered off my computer and smiled at her as she sat in the chair across from my desk.

"So what have you gotten so far? I've gotten a meeting with a radio head to see about getting a commercial slot, but that's tomorrow morning."

"I have a few bloggers who are gonna publish the piece we had Angie type up, and then they're gonna come back and give their own opinions."

"Who did you get?"

"Well one in particular is Black Tie blog."

"Oh shit."

"Yes so everything has to be on point, from the food, to the decor, to the people in attendance, because you know they're pretty brutal with new businesses."

"I do know that. Zeus will be happy to hear that they'll be in attendance."

"I'm sure," I chuckled.

"Hey so what do you think of him?"

"Of Zeus?" I quizzed and she nodded. "I think he's handsome and he's gonna be the reason my next paycheck is very nice." I giggled. "Why?"

"Just wondering. I think he is a little too flirty. I was thinking that maybe you and I can switch positions on this job. Let him flirt with you."

"Excuse me?" I laughed. "And why would you wanna put me in that position, Tati? Are you saying you can't really handle yourself?"

"No! No of course not. There is nothing another man can say or do that would make me want to leave Tef. I'm just saying, it's a little uncomfortable."

"Well tell him that. Just let him know that his flirty behavior is bothersome, and you can't work like that."

"And Eddie will kill me if I say that and lose the client."

"Eddie's ass will be fine. And he's like our father. You know he will Kung Fu Panda Zeus' ass if he thinks he's messing with one of us."

"I guess you're right. So tell me, what did Merce say about you guys being in a relationship? Is it official?"

"Yeah it is. But I don't know, I just feel down still. Has nothing to do with Calvin, he's great. It's just something feels weird."

"Hmm, why don't you talk with someone. I mean I'm here for you, always, but maybe you need a professional, Jadynn."

"Are you trying to call me crazy?" I palmed my chest, pretending to be offended.

"No, but a lot of stuff has happened to you, and sometimes you need someone you don't know to vent to. I went to a therapist after I lost the first baby."

"For real? I thought you were joking."

"Nope I really went. It helped too. So when I lost the second one, which was a bit more traumatic, I knew how to deal with it."

"Yeah by bouncing on Teflon."

"That helped too," she grinned.

"Well maybe I will, but I doubt it. I'm not the type to need counseling of any kind. I'm pretty strong."

Standing up, she leaned on my desk a little and said, "Being strong all the time can sometimes make you weaker. If you let yourself be vulnerable a few times, you'll be much more resilient, Jadynn. Trust me." She walked to the door and looked over her shoulder. "I'm going to dinner with Teflon, but if Brevin gets the balls to call you, tell him I'm working late and in a meeting so I can't talk."

"Of course. Have fun boo."

I sat there for another ten minutes, and as I stood up, Merce texted me.

Babe: *You cooking tonight?*

Me: *Uh yeah sure I guess. What do you have a taste for?*

Babe: *Pasta*

Me: *I thought you told me you didn't like pasta.*

Babe: *I don't, but yours was good as fuck. So make that and a lot so I can have thirds.*

Chuckling, I told him I would and then grabbed my purse before locking my office.

Before going to the grocery store, I decided to drop by my mother's because she'd been complaining about seeing me. I was ignoring her, until I saw this article yesterday about how this girl was sad because she hadn't talked to her mother in a while, and then she died. My mom got on my last nerves, especially with her favoritism towards Paige, but at the end of the day I did love her and I would be devastated if she passed while we weren't on speaking terms. I would be devastated even if we were speaking.

"Oh!" My mother gasped, opening the front door.

I gave a fake smile as she yanked me into my childhood home, and hugged me tightly. I grew up in this house, located in Old Brooklyn, and most times that I came over here, it felt good because it reminded me of my father.

"Ma, my neck," I groaned.

"Yes, sorry." She closed and locked the door behind me. "Sit sit sit. Would you like something to drink or eat?"

"No, I can't stay long. I have to get to the store and pick up some things to make dinner."

"Really?" She sat next to me and started running a scissor down some ribbon so it would curl. "You never cook."

"I cook all the time."

"Must be that new man I hear you've been hanging with. Paige says he's very handsome but a bad guy."

"Ma, what are you doing?" I stared down at the ribbon.

"Oh, I forgot to tell you. Russell and Paige are expecting a baby, and they're gonna have a little announcement party. The whole family is gonna be there; your aunt and cousins."

"She's having a party to announce the fact that she's pregnant? Wow." I fell back into the couch and sighed.

"You should come."

"I'm gonna pretend you didn't say that."

"What? Jadynn you should. It'd be the perfect moment for you guys to make up. And I don't want Loretta seeing that you guys are bickering. She'll just blame it on me."

Loretta was my father's sister, and for as long as I could remember she couldn't stand my mother. She felt like my mom was a pretender, always acting if things were okay when they weren't. I didn't like people disrespecting my mom, but I had to agree with Loretta. You could have a gun to my mom's head and she'd still be smiling, acting like things were all roses and sugar.

"I am not going to the party, Ma. Do you not understand that Paige slept with my boyfriend, and then that boyfriend turned around and raped me!"

Setting the ribbon and scissors down, she turned her body to face me and said, "I mean it's not like you hadn't had sex with him before, Jadynn."

"Wow, are you serious right now?" I laughed angrily.

"If it had have been some guy that you'd never been intimate with, then I could see the problem, but honestly sweetie, was it really rape? I think it was more of rough sex."

"Rough sex," I repeated lowly and looked off, staring at the old picture of my father carrying me around on his back when I was eight years old.

"Yes."

"So you don't think a man can rape a woman if he's already had sex with her? How would you feel if an ex of yours came through here and violated you, Ma?" I felt tears welling up, watching her go back to stroking the ribbon with the scissors like she hadn't said the rudest shit to me.

"Never had an old boyfriend. Only man I've been with is your father so I wouldn't mind if he came back to life and slept with me."

"Okay, I don't know why I came over here." I rose to my feet to grab my purse as she shook her head and sighed.

"You were always so dramatic. You got that from your father's side."

Without another word, I left my parents home, and got back into my car. Maybe seeing a therapist was a good idea, because I couldn't go on allowing shit to break me like this.

CHAPTER TEN

Tatiana

I'd just finished taking my nightly bath after having dinner with Teflon, and I couldn't wait to lie down and go to sleep. Tomorrow I'd scheduled off so that I could rest, and maybe catch up on a few things I could do from home.

I'd been working really hard on this opening for Zeus, and being pregnant at the same time made it more difficult. These days I was tired as hell every other hour, but my job required me to make endless phone calls, attend meetings whether it be on Skype, in person, or a phone call, and run errands. And ninety percent of the time I wanted to say fuck it all, just for a thirty-minute nap. So tomorrow was gonna be my lazy day, especially because I knew Brevin had some meetings of his own. I'd eavesdropped on his conversation, which was how I knew which day to choose.

After letting my hair air dry a little, I put some butter cream in it, and then tied it up into a curly bun on the top of my head. I slipped my silk nightshirt over my head, and then put on the matching shorts before putting my feet into my house shoes. Coming out of the bedroom, I went down the hall, passing the staircase until I made it to Suzanne's bedroom. I wanted to talk to her about what she'd seen, because I hadn't had a chance to. She must not have said anything to Brevin because I would have been dead by now I'm sure.

I knocked lightly, and when she said to come in, I opened the door and quickly closed it behind myself.

"Oh Ms. Drew. Did you need something? Dinner is ready and I was retiring for the night." She closed her robe.

"No, nothing like that I just wanted to talk to you really quickly."

"Okay sure."

"I know you saw… what you saw in the kitchen last week, and I just want you to know that, umm, that I don't mean to put you in the middle of things. I uh…"

I looked off. I didn't really know what to say. What I really wanted was to ask her to keep quiet like she'd been doing, but I didn't know what her response would be.

"I'm not going to tell, Ms. Drew, if that's what you want to know. Brevin already asked me if I felt like you guys were coming apart at the seams, and instead of telling on you, I told him to just try harder."

"Th-thank you. But can I ask why you didn't tell? I mean not that I want you to because I definitely don't, but why didn't you say anything?"

"Because I've been working here in this house for years, Ms. Drew, and I honestly have been waiting for you to leave him ever since I stepped foot inside. The things that he's put you through, he doesn't deserve you and therefore I wasn't gonna be the one to attempt to take away what little happiness you're getting. I haven't seen you float around the house like that since I was first employed."

I chuckled, covering my mouth a little bit for some reason.

"Well I appreciate that, Suzanne, I do. I'm gonna tell him, well no I'm not. I don't know how all of this is gonna end but I do love Teflon. It's not some little fling I swear."

"Oh I know darling. I can tell by the way he looks at you when he knows he can't approach you like he wants. You don't even notice sometimes. He just watches you while you eat, or when you're talking to someone else, or just reading on your tablet. Only time a man is content with just being in your presence like that and can get caught up just watching you, is when he loves you. I knew you two were in love well before the kitchen incident."

Again I smiled, thinking about what she'd said. She was right about me not noticing, because I had no idea that Teflon paid attention to me like that.

"Yes, well goodnight, Suzanne."

"Goodnight, Ms. Drew."

I left her bedroom with a smile on my face, and when I bumped into Brevin I gasped heavily, clutching my chest.

"Sorry baby. What were you doing down the hall?"

"I was umm, just talking with Suzanne."

"Talking? With the help? About what? Us?"

He seemed paranoid.

"Us? What would I be saying to Suzanne about us? And I like talking to *the help* because I want to know them better Brevin. Get off your high horse some times. And move, you smell like a bar." I nudged him and walked off briskly. He had his nerve when he was just asking Suzanne for advice.

"Tati!"

I kept it pushing until I was in the guest room. Hopefully that argument I created would keep him off of me for the night, and stop him from talking about the wedding.

***

The next day...

Teflon intruded on my day off, and forced me out of the house to get something to eat. And being pregnant, I loved food, so he didn't have to twist my arm too much. At the moment we were in Tremont, at this bar like restaurant named Bourbon Street Barrel Room. They had really good creole dishes that I never got tired of.

We both ordered the Canal Street chicken wrap along with the Luzianne iced tea. My mouth watered just thinking about it.

I felt butterflies in my stomach every time Teflon smiled at me, and I couldn't help but to grin and blush. Being with him gave me a feeling I'd never felt with Brevin, and to add to this, I was about to eat some good ass food.

"I swear knowing you got my baby inside you be having my dick on brick status all damn day." He kissed the side of my face.

"It better only be that way around me and not these Cleveland hoes out here."

"Never, you know I only have eyes for you."

"Do you think over time that will change?"

"Nah I don't. Maybe if I loved you only for your looks or something superficial like that, but what we have is deeper so I can't see my feelings for you dwindling. Shit you got me wanting to get married. You know how crazy that shit is?" He shook his head, almost talking to himself.

"I guess that potion I slipped into your orange juice that morning worked," I chuckled before he kissed me a couple times.

"Shit I'm starting to think you did do something to me. I was a player pimp, and now I'm trying to be husband and father of the year."

"Boy please, I don't have time to be tricking niggas."

"You're too pretty for that shit I know. And that pussy is on some other shit too." He bit down on his lip, and scanned my body as if it was the best one he'd ever seen.

"You always act like I have the best assets," I laughed.

"I guess I don't care about that other shit no more. It's plenty of muthafuckas out here with double D's and huge asses, but they also got a dick between their legs."

"Ugh, I don't wanna think about that." I turned my lip up, slightly chuckling.

"Shit me either."

"I was thinking about getting my breasts done. Maybe after the baby, I would get like a nice C cup or even a small D."

"For what? Don't do that shit for *me*. If you get that make sure it's for you. I love the way your body looks and I don't need all that shit. But if you'd feel more comfortable getting it, then okay."

"So you're telling me you wouldn't prefer some nice jugs sitting here instead of these?" I cheesed, pointing to my boobs. I had on a top that looked like a bikini top, and flared out a little under the breast area.

"Nope." His eyes gazed lustfully at them before he leaned in to kiss my neck. His hand ran up my thigh, and he groped it roughly.

"Okay we have two Canal chicken wraps, and two iced teas!" a lady came over with our food, prompting me to nudge Teflon's freaky ass off of me.

"Thank you," I replied.

We ate our food, and then ordered the Bourbon Bread Pudding for dessert. After scarfing that down, my bladder was going crazy, so I got up to go the bathroom. Once I relieved myself, I came out to wash my hands. As I was doing so, someone walked in and I saw it was Amanda, Brevin's baby mama.

"Well hello," she smiled.

"I'm not in the mood, and you're not in the condition, so please let's skip the conversation for today."

"Oh of course, I wouldn't want to keep you from the guy you're cheating on Brevin with. He's fine as fuck though. How do you get so many men?"

"Fuck you."

Laughing she said, "I always knew you were a hoe. But for some reason Brevin likes that hot box that everyone else has probably been in."

WHAM!

Out of reflex, I slapped the shit out of her. She slowly turned to look at me, and began laughing once again while caressing her belly.

"Move." I pushed past her and yanked the bathroom door open.

"What do you think Brevin will say when I ask him about you fucking another man?" she called after me.

I paused for a moment, but then just kept walking. Maybe Brevin finding out would be for the best. I was tired of hiding, and even more tired of playing his woman.

CHAPTER ELEVEN

Teflon

I placed some cash on the table for the bill and the tip, and as I put the knot back into my pocket, I looked up to see Tatiana storming towards the table. Frowning, I was about to ask her what was wrong, but she snatched her purse up and started towards the door so I followed.

"Aye, what's— what the fuck is wrong with you?" I gripped her arm, and when she snatched it I gripped her little ass up again.

"Let me go! We have to leave before that bitch comes out!"

"What bitch?" I hollered.

Tatiana looked around a little at the people walking into the bar and some going past it, before she exhaled heavily.

"The girl that Brevin got pregnant is here and she's gonna tell Brevin that she saw us together, Tef."

"Come on." I led her to the car, which was parked across the street, and after helping her into the passenger seat, I went around to my side and got in. "What does she look like?"

"Why?"

"Just tell me. I want to see her when she comes out."

"Skinny, huge breasts, an even bigger belly and a flat ass. She's shaped like a toothbrush," she pouted, making me laugh.

"Does she really look like that or are you just hating?"

"No, that's how she looks. She has long brown hair as well, with red tips on it that are fried and look horrible."

"Aight."

We sat there in the car, and I felt Tatiana look at me a few times. She sighed, and then typed away on her phone for a few moments.

"Baby what are we doing?" I didn't respond as I eyed the entrance of the restaurant we were just in, waiting for that bitch she'd just described to me. "Tre'Wayne!"

"I'm waiting for old girl to bring her snitching ass out."

"Why are—"

The cranking of my car cut her off and damn was I thankful. I watched the girl approach her car, so I looked to Tatiana who nodded to confirm that was her. She was parked in front of the restaurant, so when she pulled off towards College Avenue, I followed her ass.

"What are we doing?" Tatiana quizzed.

"Going to have a little talk with her."

"Oh my gosh."

We followed her ass all the way to some house on Forest Avenue in Buckeye-Shaker, and I parked right behind her stupid ass. I waited until she got out of the car, and once she was up at her door, I got out and hiked up her porch stairs, prompting her to turn right the fuck around.

"How are you?" I smiled, leaning up against the balcony part of her porch.

"What do you want?" she frowned.

"I just wanted to make sure that you had no plans on opening yo' hoe ass mouth to that bitch you're pregnant by."

"And if I do?"

"Then I'll get rid of you when I get rid of him."

Laughing, she clapped her hands together, and then folded her arms over her saggy ass tits.

"I'll be sure to let Brevin know— ah!" she gasped when I gripped her jaw and squeezed it tightly. She whimpered in pain as I pressed her up against the screen, still holding her face.

"Teflon!" Tatiana yelped, getting out of the car.

"Get back in!" I roared, and she did exactly what I'd told her to. Turning my attention back to this bitch in front of me I said, "I'm only gon' say this one more muthafuckin' time bitch, keep yo' mouth shut about what you saw, or I'm smoking yo' ass right along with that nigga."

She nodded her head up and down before saying, "Okay." It was a struggle for her to speak because I was grasping her jaw so tightly. If I squeezed any harder it would probably snap.

"When I let you go, do not run in there and phone him because I'll have a bullet through ya dome before the line finishes ringing."

Again she nodded, so I let her go. Walking back to the car, I slipped in and waited until she went back in the house.

"Do you think she will be quiet?"

"I don't know, but if she isn't I'm killing her."

I could feel Tatiana's worried eyes settle on me as I cranked up the car. I hated to talk like that in front of her, but any muthafucka that tried to get in the way of me protecting her was going down, pregnant or not.

I drove quickly back to Brevin's house so that Tatiana and I could split up before he made it home, and once I hit the corner of his street, I pulled over, kissed her, and then got out of the car so I could walk the rest of the way. She obviously made it before me, so when I got inside she was on the couch watching TV already, setting out snacks.

"Baby— Tati didn't you just eat?" I whispered with a smile.

"Yes, but this is just a snack," she smiled, sitting down on the couch and turning up one of them stupid ass reality shows.

I watched her stuff her face and enjoy that bullshit show for a little bit, knowing that I couldn't wait to be able to touch her whenever the fuck I felt like it.

As soon as I got into the bedroom I called my own, I checked my phone since it'd been buzzing and doing all kinds of shit since Tatiana and I left the restaurant. I was too focused on hemming up that bitch that I didn't care to pay attention to it. When I looked, I saw Merce sent me a message within the burner app.

Merce: Ready for phase two after tonight?

Me: Of course.

Right after I hit send, my mother's name popped up to let me know she was calling. I was sleepy as hell, and wanted to take a quick nap before Merce and Brevin came back since I was on trap duty tonight, but I couldn't ignore my mama.

"Hey pretty." I turned on my back and groaned, throwing my forearm across my eyes.

"Hi son, can you come over please?"

"Uh, yeah I'll come through there in a few hours or maybe tomorrow if I don't have time to do so today."

"Oh because I was thinking right now."

"Ma, nah I'm really tired. I just ate a big meal and I'm working long hours tonight."

"Please! I have a nice surprise for you honey. You're gonna love it and it's gonna wake you right up. Plus sleeping after eating will only make you fat."

"Uh, alright. Give me like twenty minutes and it better be worth it ma. Have some food ready for me too."

"I will."

Once we hung up, I grunted out of frustration because I was so tired. I was mentally and physically exhausted, and just needed some sleep. Sleep was the only time that my mind was at ease.

After staring off through the window in my bedroom that showed the backyard, I stood up and rolled my neck to get any kinks out, then grabbed my keys and phone. I tried to dart through the living area, but Tatiana saw me and of course wanted to know where I was going.

"Just to see what my mom needs baby, that's it."

"Why haven't I met her yet?"

"I… I don't know, Tati. A lot of shit has been going on and I guess I just didn't think about it. She wants to meet you though so it'll be soon aight?" She nodded somberly, so I moved closer to her and kissed her gently. "I swear you're gonna meet her, Tatiana. I gotta go though."

The faster I got to my mother's the quicker I could see this surprise then get back to Brevin's for a few minutes of shut eye.

I finally made to my mom's crib in Corlett, on Ferris avenue. I pulled over right in front, and then hopped out, hitting the alarm as I jogged up her walkway. I hit the stairs, and before I even made it to the door good, I was beating on it like the police.

"Alright alright!" I heard her yell from behind the door, just before the sound of her twisting the locks could be heard. "Baby!" she grinned, coming out of the worn out screen door and locking her arms around my neck.

"Hey, ma." I backed her into the house as she held onto my neck still. Her ass could be so over the top. She didn't even act this way when I first brought my ass back from California. As I put her down I asked, "What was the surprise yo—"

"She the only person in this room that you know?" my little brother Thomas grinned, walking into the living room from the back.

"Oh shit!" I cheesed, walking over to embrace him. "I missed you man. When the fuck did you get back?" I backed from him, looking him over to make sure he was intact. I wouldn't mind flying to France to fuck somebody up for messing with him.

"Just last night. I told Ma not to tell you yet, because I wanted it to be a surprise."

"Shit," I panted, smiling. I missed my little brother like crazy.

I was always his protector, so him being without me in another country worried me a lot. It was different when he was in Ohio and I was in California, because at least he had Groove and my mother even. But I don't know shit about how them French niggas get down.

"Hey, Teflon," Thomas' girlfriend Cameron walked into the living room.

"Sup." I hugged her before everyone sat down, except my mom who said she'd made some refreshments.

"So how was France? Did you see anything nice?" I laughed, and Cameron shot me a look. "I mean like the art and shit."

Chuckling, Thomas replied, "Yeah right nigga. You couldn't stick with one woman if somebody paid you. But yeah there was a lot of nice stuff. You should go for sure."

"Don't insult my baby. He's a changed man now, Thomas." My mom walked back in with a tray of green iced tea and some snacks she'd prepared, then set it on the table.

"Changed?" Thomas grabbed one of the cookies and bit it.

"Yes, tell them, Tre'Wayne! Tell them about *Tatiana*."

"Ooh *Tatiana!* Sounds exotic," Cameron and Thomas chuckled in unison.

"Tatiana is my girlfriend. I don't really know what else to say." I nodded, giving my mom a playful glare.

"He's in love, Thomas."

"In love?"

"Come on Ma, damn! I mean dang." I frowned.

"Wow… Teflon in love. I have to meet this Tatiana," Cameron sipped her iced tea and sat back in the big recliner, smiling along with everyone else.

"He'll bring her by soon, but right now it's complicated. She's engaged to another man, however she and Teflon fell into a whirlwind romance and now they're in love!" my mom dramatically explained, telling every got damn thing I'd told her. "My baby swept her right off her feet. She couldn't resist his charm, and now she's conflicted!"

"You should write books, Mrs. German," Cameron nodded as my mother grinned at the compliment.

"Don't hype her," Thomas shook his head. "But aye I would love to meet her. I don't know about that engaged part because it sounds like she's using you for a phase she's going through, but I will have to see."

"Well she's not. I know this for sure."

"Good," Thomas nodded.

CHAPTER TWELVE

Brevin

The next evening…

"Aye are you ready to go?" I peeked into the room Teflon stayed in to see him cleaning up or doing whatever the fuck he was doing.

"Go where?" he frowned, tossing the folded clothes onto the bed.

"I'm going over to Mack's house real brief. Nigga wants to talk and I have some shit to go over with him. But first I wanna stop by Garrett's because we'll be at Mack's longer."

"I thought Merce was going."

"Yeah I need y'all both."

He stared at me for a little bit like he wanted to say something, then he chuckled lightly and nodded.

"Aight let me put this shit up and we can roll out."

"Thanks." I moved from his door and mumbled, "Bitch ass nigga."

I hated feeling like the people who worked for me felt like I did stupid shit, but I needed Teflon's insubordinate ass at the moment. But once whomever was terrorizing my traps had been handled, I was letting that nigga go.

About ten minutes went by before the three of us were leaving. We headed to see Garrett first in Detroit-Shoreway, because I wanted to put him on trap duty along with Teflon and Merce. I had a feeling that someone had caught onto the fact that I had them two watching, so they were following them and waiting for them to leave before attacking the traps. By saying that, I was gonna have Garrett come by whatever trap Teflon, Merce, or Groove had just left and possibly catch the culprit.

"So this is where G lives?" Merce quizzed me as Teflon pulled up.

"Yep."

"How much you paying him?" Teflon frowned as both he and Merce eyed the big home.

"Enough, why?"

"I don't know I guess I expected something better. Maybe he just likes to live humbly," Teflon replied, shutting the engine off.

Garrett and Mack got paid whatever the fuck I wanted to pay them and that was it. Shit the nigga had a house and he should be happy about it. Matter fact he must have been cool with the house because he'd yet to complain. Only muthafucka complaining was Teflon's ass.

We walked up the porch steps, and I yanked the screen door open before using an open palm to beat on the door. No one answered, so I twisted the knob to see the door was unlocked. Garrett was one of them niggas who thought they were invincible, and didn't take certain safety precautions. That shit annoyed me sometimes, but it worked in my favor when I needed him to do shit that I didn't feel doing.

"Garrett!" I shouted through the house as Teflon and Merce followed me in. "Y'all can sit down," I turned to look back at them.

"Uh nah I'm good," Merce scanned the dirty ass couches, one with a banana peel and an old smashed sandwich on it.

"Yeah umm, me too," I said as we all chuckled. "Garrett!"

"Aight man damn!" he barked from the back bedroom, before snatching the door open and coming out. "I ain't know you were coming through this early." He snatched up some newspaper from one of his couches and sat down.

"I told you a little after 4pm, and it's 6:45pm nigga." I checked my Cartier. "I'm actually hella late." I shook my head.

"Oh my bad, y'all can sit down."

"Nah we good," Teflon and Merce replied almost simultaneously, and Garrett just nodded.

Shortly after, when I was about to speak, some dude came from the same bedroom Garrett was in, looking just as suspicious and frazzled as Garret had looked a few minutes ago.

"Sup, Brev." He reached his hand out to shake mine and I looked down at it with disgust.

"Fuck up outta my face nigga."

The dude just nodded, glanced at Garrett and said, "I'll holla at you later, G."

"Why are you locked up in a bedroom with another nigga G? You know what, I don't even wanna fucking know right now. I just came to tell you that I need you on another shift of trap duty."

"Aight which one?"

"Only one trap left," Teflon reminded me.

"Damn for real?" I looked to him. "Them niggas got all the other four?"

"Yeah, they did." Merce nodded.

"Fuck! Okay calm down, Brevin." I told myself, massaging my temples. "Aight look it needs to be watched around the fucking clock. I have to go see Mack in a few, but go watch it now, and then later tonight Groove can push through there. Tef you'll get the morning, Merce you're next, then Garrett, and then Groove. I'll let y'all know the day after that who will be watching and when. I have some shit to handle and I might need Teflon and or Merce to come with me."

"Aight," Garrett nodded.

"Nigga I said now! What the fuck you still sitting here for huh? Get yo' ass up and get ready to go!" I roared, prompting him to hop up and search frantically for his shoes.

I shoved the screen door open and walked out with Teflon and Merce behind me. We got inside of the car, and Teflon started off towards Mack's house.

"Aye so you know them two was fucking right?" Merce chuckled along with Teflon.

"I don't even wanna think about the shit. Nigga got a baby mama down in West Virginia who up and left his ass, and niggas didn't know why. I'm pretty sure that was the reason," I shook my head, looking out the window since it was getting darker now.

We made it to Mack's home which was much cleaner, and went into the den so I could explain the same get down that was gonna be happening. Both Garrett and Mack were supposed to have the same positions, but Mack was smarter so I didn't have him getting his hands dirty like Garrett.

After I told him the houses were gonna be watched and how, Mack asked me to come speak with him in another room.

"You good?" I folded my arms once we got to his kitchen.

"Actually nah I'm not good. Gloria is pregnant my nigga."

"And?"

"Fuck do you mean and?"

"What the fuck does her hoe ass being pregnant got to do with me?"

"A lot since you've been fucking her. Look I'm not saying it's definitely yo' damn baby because it could be mine, but I'm letting you know."

"I don't need this shit right now!" I hollered, slamming my fist onto the counter. I ran my hand down my face, before locking my hands on top of my head. "Fuck! I already got Amanda coming at me with this baby shit, and now possibly Gloria. Fuck! Fuck! Fuck!" I kicked the shit out of his dishwasher until it had a dent in it. "I uh, I gotta go, Mack. Tell her ass to get an abortion or something."

"Nah because it could be mine."

"Well if it turns out not to be, you taking care of the muthafucka because I damn sure won't be! So it's up to you, do you wanna play daddy to a kid that ain't yours, or would you rather just be smart and kill the one inside of her to be sure you don't have to? It's your choice. Don't be stupid my nigga."

I looked at him for a little bit, seeing the wheels turning in his head. I honestly didn't want Gloria to have this baby because I was sure I'd fucked her more than Mack, so it was more likely my kid than not. I didn't love Gloria, just like I didn't love Amanda, and didn't want them bringing kids into this world. How is it that God would allow babies to be born from some stupid cum bucket ass hoes, but not from my own girl? Kind of shit is that?

"You aight?" Merce quizzed when I made it to the entrance area of the den.

"Ye-yeah I'm good. Let's get up out of here." I turned on my heels and they followed. As we passed Mack in the kitchen, he was inspecting his dishwasher, but then rose to his feet to look at me. "Be smart my nigga," was all I said before leaving out.

I called home on the way there to make sure Suzanne had dinner in rotation, and once she told me she did, I was cool. I was hungrier than a muthafucka and wanted to walk through that door and chow down. Next I called Tatiana, who picked up on the fourth ring.

"Where are you?" I questioned before she could speak.

"I'm just leaving work, why?"

"Because I'm your man and I need to know where the fuck you are at all times. You've been coming home too late and I ain't with that shit."

I saw Teflon look at me through his rearview mirror, as I spoke. When we made eye contact, he looked away. He was way too worried about Tatiana for my liking; another reason I was letting his ass go once the smoke had cleared.

"Baby I told you I had a big client that I needed to tend to."

"Well I need you to tend to something else tonight. Go straight home, Tatiana and I'm not fucking around with you."

"I am, I am… Brevin."

She paused before saying my name almost like she forgot the shit, or like she had to remind herself who she was talking to.

"Good." Was all I said before hanging up.

I had Teflon stop at the store so I could get some Hennessy, and then we went back to the house. I saw Tatiana's car parked there, and nodded approvingly. As we walking in I unscrewed the top on my drink and took a long swig as I entered the kitchen to see what Suzanne had made. When I spotted Tatiana at the stove with her, smiling and talking, I came up behind her and hugged her little body.

"You smell so fucking good," I spoke against her ear.

"Brevin," she whined, as I hugged her tightly, pressing my hard dick against her. I noticed Teflon and Merce watching as they sat down at the table, ready to eat.

"Let's get a quickie in," I whispered to her.

"I'm hungry, Brevin. Maybe after."

"Nah I need some attention now." I lifted her using one arm, and took down some more Hennessy with my free hand as I carried her to the guest room on the side.

"Brevin, baby I'm really hungry. Let me eat first," she begged when I placed her to her feet and locked the door. "I need energy."

"Don't need no energy." I set my bottle on the dresser and then wiped my mouth with the back of my hand before unbuckling my jeans. "I ain't touched you in decades, all you gotta do is lie there."

"Brevin please."

I pushed her onto her back, and when she tried to get up, I got in between her legs. She was way too small to fight me off, so it was in her best interest to give up now.

I pinned her hands to the bed, and started kissing on her neck as she whined and whimpered.

"Aye shut the fuck up, Tati! Why you even acting like this?" I frowned as she looked up at me. "I got needs and you need to fulfill them if you're gonna be my bitch."

"Then we can break up!"

"Yeah we can, and then I can kill you."

Her chest heaved up and down as she scowled. She wasn't intimidating in the least, so the shit was comical.

Putting both of her wrists into one hand, I used my other to reach between her legs to rip her panties.

"Brevin stop! I don't want to!"

BOOM! BOOM!

"The fuck?" I looked over my shoulder at he door to see that someone was trying to kick the shit in. It was denting, and then soon enough a whole was in it, and I saw Teflon reach through to unlock it.

"Tef!" Merce hollered after him as he barged into the room.

WHAM! WHAM!

I felt like my neck was gonna snap with how powerful the punches were that Teflon threw my way. I couldn't think straight for a few moments as I tried to stop all the damn blood coming from my nose.

Seeing Tatiana hop from the bed and hide behind Teflon told me something I didn't want to know; she and this nigga had a thing. The way he looked at me with that deranged expression, like he wanted to murder me for touching her, told me he wasn't only fucking my bitch, but he loved her.

"I'm done with this fake shit!" Teflon shouted as I tried to get my dizzy ass together. "Done! Fuck him and all this bullshit!"

"Tef—"

"I said I'm done!" he barked at Merce. "Tatiana let's go! Get whatever the fuck you need and come on right now!" he darted out and she ran right behind him.

That was the last thing I saw before I blacked out…

CHAPTER THIRTEEN

Merce

"Shit," I grumbled, rushing to the room I stayed in to gather the little shit I kept over here.

Teflon had completely ruined the fucking plan, but I couldn't say I blamed him. Tatiana was his girl, and he couldn't continue to stand by and watch some nigga treat her any kind of way. Come to think of it, I couldn't imagine having to do that, so being mad at him because he snapped wasn't some shit I was about to do.

Once I had all my belongings shoved into my big duffle bag, I went down the hall and saw Teflon come out at the same time. He gave me a look and shook his head, adjusting his bag on his shoulder.

"It's cool man we gon' figure this shit out," I told him, not wanting him to worry. "I'll get at Groove and see what we can do."

He nodded and then we headed towards the kitchen where Tatiana was waiting for him, dressed in one of his jackets. She slipped her hand into his, and as we walked by, Suzanne gave us a warm smile. I thought that was odd because I just knew for sure she was dedicated to Brevin's cause; whatever it was.

"You knocked him out cold, Teflon. I'll get him straight but I will let you guys leave first," Suzanne said.

"Thanks," I replied since Teflon was on a mission to leave.

They both got into Tatiana's car, and then I got into mine after throwing my bag in the backseat. I texted Jadynn to let her know I wanted to see her tonight and would be picking her up, then I peeled out of the driveway.

The plan was to go straight to Jadynn, but since shit hit the fan tonight I wanted to make a stop. We planned to wait shit out before getting at Mack, but it was now or never. And from the look on his face when we left his crib earlier, whatever conversation he'd had with Brevin must not have went too well.

Once I got to Mack's, I parked the rental I'd been using, and then went up to his door. His bitch answered, and when she saw me she licked her lips sensually. She was a straight up and down hoe. It didn't matter who you were, if you had a little bread she'd be willing.

"Aye is Mack here?"

"Yeah, what you need him for?"

"Don't worry about all that ma, I just need to speak with him. Can I come in?"

"What you gonna do for me?" she cocked her head and smiled.

"Get the fuck out my way." I yanked the screen door open and barged in past her stupid hoe ass.

"Hey! Excuse you nigga!"

I ignored her as I went past the kitchen and to the den where I found Mack sitting down on the couch holding a beer. He looked like his whole world had been shattered, and as fucked up as it may have sounded, that was perfect. I needed him to be in low spirits, ready to team up with us so we could take Brevin out. Brevin was the head of everything, but Mack was the main connection to the team. If an order was to be followed, Mack delivered the message.

He could have turned the whole squad against Brevin ages ago, but he was not only a bitch, he was stupid as fuck too. Nigga was also too loyal. I didn't know there was a such thing until I ran across him. But any nigga that talks shit to me and fucks my girl is not getting my respect, and that's what Mack failed to realize.

"Hey man," I spoke up, shoving my hands into my jean pockets.

"Oh hey, what's up? Brevin aight?"

This nigga.

Stepping further into the den, I looked to see what he had on television before nodding my head. I tapped my waist to be sure I had my piece, just in case our conversation went left and he tried to jump bad with me.

"Yeah he's straight," I lied. Sitting down on the other end of the couch I asked, "But how are you? You good?"

Shrugging he replied, "I'm whatever." He kept his eyes on the TV as he took a swig of beer and then started coughing.

"Aye so I wanted to talk to you about something."

"What's up?" he finally looked my way. "Oh did you want a beer?

Gloria can bring you—"

"Nah I'm good." I cleared my throat. "But aye honestly, since I been here, Brevin ain't been doing shit but spending money, fucking hoes, drinking, and laying up all day. You do all the damn work, so I'm just wondering why is he the nigga barking out orders?"

"He's just been having a bad year. He's usually more on his shit. I think Mook and Tone getting shot kind of fucked his head up."

Laughing I said, "Damn you really are loyal as fuck. I mean you do all the work and let this nigga smash your bitch, and you still don't talk down about him."

Mack stared off for a moment, drumming his fingertips against the beer bottle before taking another sip.

"She's pregnant."

"Who?" my brows furrowed.

"Gloria man," he scoffed. "He got my bitch pregnant," his voice trembled and I bucked my eyes when he wasn't looking.

Was this muthafucka about to cry? Over a hoe? That bitch would have been lucky to be alive if I found out she was busting her shit open for another nigga, let alone my homie. And then pregnant? Her dead body would have been lying in my yard.

"Damn man that's fucked up. You sure it's his?"

"I mean I don't know, but she's saying according to the timing it's his." Chuckling angrily he added, "She's been letting him fuck more than me, so shit. And what can I say; it's her body. She knows it better than either of us." He took another swallow of the beer. Before he could even finish swallowing he said, "But I low-key don't even give a fuck no more. All these hoes are the same out here in Ohio."

"If it makes you feel any better, you got Teflon's and my support if you want to dethrone this nigga. He ain't doing shit but fucking the people over that have been there for his ass. I mean look at the way he treats his girl. If he'll whoop her little ass like she's a nigga and not miss a beat, you shouldn't be surprised by the fact that he don't give a shit about his homies."

"Hmm, so what you saying?" He looked over at me.

"I'm saying lets pull the rug from under his ass. Let's show that nigga that he can't go on fucking niggas over."

"I don't know, Merce. I mean, Brevin is my main man."

"Yeah and he fucked yo' girl. Nigga didn't even try to hide it from you. That shows just how much he *doesn't* respect you. He's blatantly fucking yo' bitch, because he knows deep down you ain't gon' do shit about it," I gassed him up.

Scratching his head, he placed his beer bottle on the coffee table and sat back, thinking. He sighed heavily, and then looked my way.

"I do know everything about the empire. It would be nothing for me to have him thrown out on his ass. I need to think about that shit though."

"You do that. But to be honest with you, you don't wanna go against Teflon and me. If you go back and tell about this conversation, I can assure you that you'll be sleeping with the fishes soon, right along with Brevin."

"How you gon' threaten me while trying to get me on your team?"

"I ain't threatening you, I'm letting you know how shit is gonna go if you try to cross me. So yeah I'll give you time to think, no problem, but if you play me I'm smoking you and that's on my mama."

"Nah I hear you," he nodded. "I get it. And who knows, I may get you first."

"We'd just have to see then." I rose to my feet. "So I'll be in touch or vice versa, aight?"

"Yep."

We slapped hands and then I left his crib so I could pick up my girl.

When we got to my spot, I heard rap music coming from the room my little brother Sebastian stayed in, and started to go back there but Jadynn grabbed my arm.

"What?" I looked at her.

"Just let him be. Plus, it's better if he doesn't hear us tonight right?"

Smiling I responded, "You sure know how to get a nigga to do what the fuck you want him to do."

She giggled as I led her to my bedroom and closed the door behind us.

"So I was thinking about going to see a psychologist." She took her jacket off and then her shoes before looking at me for a response.

"Uh, for what baby?"

"I don't know, just to have someone to talk to I guess. Why, do you think it's stupid?"

"Not stupid, just… I don't know I guess I've never known anyone who needed a therapist. You can talk to me though."

"I know baby, but Tatiana thinks it'd be better if I talked to someone who didn't know me and I think she's kind of right."

"Won't hurt to try it." I fell onto my bed, feeling tired as hell.

"Same thing I said. So why are we staying here tonight? Got tired of sleeping at Brevin's house?" she straddled my back and started to massage my shoulders. Shit felt so damn good that I closed my eyes.

"Well Teflon snapped when Brevin tried to fuck Tatiana tonight, so the plan has hit a bit of a snag."

"You serious? So what now? Brevin is gonna depopulate the city of Cleveland over Tatiana." She climbed off me and sat to the side, staring down at my face. "She's never even looked at another guy while with him and for good reason."

"I know I know, but Teflon loves her and we can't expect him to just watch her go through shit for play play. We'll come out on top, I just don't know how quite yet."

"I hope so."

Licking my lips I said, "Don't worry." I gripped her and yanked her body down so I could climb on top of her. "Just worry about this right here." I kissed her slowly while pressing my erection against her pussy.

CHAPTER FOURTEEN

Jadynn

I'd luckily found a doctor less than 20 minutes away from my place downtown, so I scheduled a visit before I had to go to work. I let Eddie know that I would be in about two hours late, because I wasn't sure how much time the psychiatrist needed. I hoped this wouldn't take long, and even prayed that I only needed one visit; it wasn't exactly the cheapest.

I finally made it to the building, and parked my car a little ways down in the back of the parking lot. I wasn't sure why, but I didn't really want anyone to know that I was here to seek help with my mental. I guess because it was a thing that black people didn't do. I was sort of embarrassed, so getting in and out of here without being seen was the definite goal.

Hurrying inside, I quickly found the floor the doctor was on, and rode the elevator up. Thankfully no one was really inside the waiting room of her suite, so I didn't have to worry about what people thought of me. After I let the receptionist know I was here, I took a seat and just looked around the office. It wasn't too much of anything to look at though; white walls, brown chairs, and white tile flooring. There were a few health and fitness magazines that I really had no interest in reading. Staring at the no cell phone sign, I retrieved my iPhone from my purse, and opened it to occupy my time. I didn't understand why phones weren't allowed but I wasn't abiding by that rule today.

"Good morning, Jemma," some lady walked in smiling.

"Morning, Helena, how are you feeling today?" the receptionist smiled back as I watched them out the corner of my eye.

"I'm good, but I'll be better after my session I'm sure."

"Yes of course. Well have a seat and you can come back in a little bit alright?"

Helena nodded with a smile and then turned halfway to scan the area for a seat. When she found one, near me of course, she made her way over and sat down.

"You must be new," she sighed, grinning widely enough for me to see she had all of her teeth.

"Uh, what do you survey the waiting room every time you come?" I chuckled awkwardly. I wasn't trying to be rude but damn how much did she come here if she knew I was new.

"Pretty much. I come four times a week and I usually see the same people all the time. But you're a new face; a beautiful one might I add."

"Well thank you."

"Helena." She stuck her hand out, hovering over my phone screen so that I had no choice but to recognize it.

"Jadynn." I shook it.

"Beautiful name. Say what are you here for, Jadynn?"

"Isn't that personal? You wouldn't want to tell someone what you were here for would you?" I frowned a little, weirded out a bit.

"No actually I don't mind." She tossed her red hair back. "I had some problems letting a relationship go, and well I came here to help me through that. To be honest I was kind of embarrassed at first."

"Well I'm glad you were able to overcome your problem, Helena. But I still don't feel comfortable telling you why I'm here. Maybe when I get to your point of recovery, I'll be more open."

"Maybe!" she sighed happily and scanned the waiting room while cupping her knees. I watched her side profile for a bit, and she turned to regain eye contact. "So have you always lived in Cleveland?"

"Ms. Davidsen, I'm ready for you." Dr. Courtney Larney smiled as she held the door open that led to the back.

Saved by the damn bell, I thought.

"Great."

I hopped up and followed her to the back, and we made it to this really nice spacious office. I spotted the leather bed like chair, and chuckled because it was just like the movies. Her wall was decorated with awards and degrees, and her desk was covered in pictures of her family. She seemed pretty normal, so I wasn't as afraid of her like before.

"Have a seat right there, Ms. Davidsen." She gestured towards the couch instead of the bed-like chair.

"Oh yes okay."

There was a coffee table in front of it, so she sat across from me in of the chairs so we could face one another. She pulled out this wooden thing, then removed her pad from it, along with a pen. She looked to be about fifty, with her short blond hair, semi wrinkled skin, and frail body. Her perfume was strong, but it was nice nonetheless.

"So how are you today?" she picked her head up from writing and smiled so big I'm sure it hurt her cheeks.

"I'm good, thanks." I re-crossed my legs. "How are you?"

"Oh I'm fine. Nothing like feeding off the problems of others." We stared at one another for a bit before she said, "I'm kidding, Ms. Davidsen."

"Oh," I exhaled. "Yeah I-I know." I smiled shyly.

"So for this session I just want to get a sense of who you are and a little summary of why you think you need my help." She pushed her glasses up, and rested her clasped hands on her legal pad.

"Well my name is Jadynn," I chuckled subtly. "I have one sister, I'm the younger one, and she's more of the favorite. When my dad was alive I kind of didn't mind because he liked me more I guess; or at least that's what I thought. Anyway, after my dad died, we got closer but my mom's favoritism over her kind of messed things up a bit."

"Okay so that's why you're here? To help you better your relationship with your sister?"

"No, no. See my sister went behind my back and started dating my boyfriend."

"Oh, okay," she started writing something.

"Yes and after they let everyone know they were gonna be together, he ca-came by the umm apartment we used to share; my apartment. And when he came he…" I fidgeted, not even wanting to remember what happened that day. "We got into a little argument and it ended with him ra— forcing himself on me… I'm sorry," I chuckled as I dabbed my eyes.

"No, don't apologize sweetheart." She reached for a tissue and handed it to me. "So your now ex boyfriend, forced himself on you *after* outing his relationship with your sister?"

"Yes." I sniffled.

"I find that very strange that he would feel the need to violate you, or have any type of contact with you if he wants to be with your sister." She scribbled as she spoke. "Sounds like he was lashing out at you because he'd realized he'd made a mistake. Now tell me, did you press charges?"

"No but I had a friend who found out and beat him up pretty badly," I laughed and sniffled. "But no I didn't go to the police."

"This friend is male right?" she inquired and I nodded. "And you guys are just friends?"

"Well we were at that time, but now he's my boyfriend."

"Okay it's good that you are still able to build relationships with males, Jadynn. A lot of times rape survivors, shut themselves off from relationships for some years." She gave me a closed mouth smile. "Is there a reason why you didn't call the authorities?"

"Just didn't want to be humiliated. I didn't need all of Cleveland knowing he raped me and I just wanted to forget about all of that."

"Understandable."

After an hour and a half, my session was over. She wanted me to come back, and even though I hadn't planned to at first, I agreed. It did feel good to talk to someone else other than Merce, Tatiana, and my mother. Not that Tatiana and Merce weren't helpful, it's just I felt like I could really peel away the layers with this random woman.

As I approached my car in the parking lot, I saw the whole hood of my car was covered in a brown substance. When I got closer, the smell almost knocked me on my ass.

"Yeah some young girl came by and spread a bucket of what looks like shit on your car," this middle aged white guy with a scruffy blond beard walked by. He shoved a toothpick into his mouth, and then slipped his hands into his dingy blue jeans to wait for my response.

"And you didn't think to maybe tell anyone in the lobby or something?" I bucked my eyes and threw my hands out.

"No," he shrugged and started off, allowing his clunky brown boots to kick up gravel.

"Asshole," I mumbled.

I gazed down at the nasty shit on my car for a few moments, wondering who the fuck would have done something like this. Then I remembered Merce telling me his ex Savannah may be starting some shit, and I guess he was serious.

Yanking my car door open, I climbed inside, cranked it up, and then drove to her house. I'd demanded the address from Merce when he gave me that heads up, just in case she did something. I honestly never thought I'd need it because a lot of bitches out here were all bark and no bite, but I guess I was gonna have to show Ms. Savannah that I wasn't the one.

Pulling up to her house, I parked in her damn driveway like I paid the bills in that bitch, and then changed out of my heels and into my sneakers that I kept in the trunk. I grabbed a metal bar that came from some shower caddy I'd failed at building and was supposed to return, then slammed my trunk back closed.

Walking over to what I assumed was her car, I swung as hard as I could, and shattered her back window. Only two seconds went by before she was coming out of her house screaming.

When she neared me, I turned to her with the bar and said, "You got me fucked up bitch. I will kill you and make sure no one ever finds your body. I'm not one of these little airheads that just run and cry to their man when a bitch fucks with them. I'll beat you and Calvin's ass if I have to and trust me, you don't want to take me there!"

"You're gonna pay for my window!"

"Yeah just as soon as you lick every drop of this shit off the hood of my car." I walked back towards my vehicle. Pulling the door open I said, "This is the first and final warning, the next time I'll be shoving this up that misshapen ass you're rocking."

I got into my car, threw the bar into the passenger seat, and stared at that hoe as I cranked my car up. She panted heavily, allowing her chest to rise and fall, before turning to look at her smashed in window. Chuckling, I sped out and headed to the carwash so I could get it cleaned. Guess I would be hitting the car wash before work.

CHAPTER FIFTEEN

Tatiana

"Leaving?"

I came out of the shower, wrapped in a towel to see Teflon dressed. Nothing major, just jeans, a t-shirt, and some all black Adidas. His black hat was pulled down low, but you could still see his sexy slanted eyes that he'd inherited from his Vietnamese mother. His smooth brown skin was lickable, adorned with a few meaningful tattoos going down his strong arms. His silver chain and matching watch complemented the simple fit perfectly. He moved towards me, allowing me to inhale the sweet masculine scent of his cologne, and as he eyed me he stroked his neatly trimmed beard. Sexy, fine, handsome, none of those words were good enough to describe how gorgeous this man was, and I was happy to say he was mine.

"Yeah, gotta handle some shit." He turned his hat to the back to expose his face, and when he tucked his sexy lips in to gaze down at me lustfully, I felt a tingle down below. "Aye where you think you going though?"

"I needed to go to the bank and the grocery store before my

meeting this evening, Tre'Wayne," I stated sternly.

He turned me around and bent me over his bed, before removing my towel and tossing it to the floor. I giggled as his hands caressed my back, butt, and legs, before his fingers began to toy with my clit. I listened to him unbuckle his jeans, and bit down on my lip as he forced his way inside of me.

"Ahh," I whimpered lowly as he began to pump me from behind.

He lifted me by my stomach so that my ass was in the air, and then continued to glide in and out of me with precision. I could feel my middle become wetter and wetter with every plunge, and soon enough my pelvic area was tingling and releasing my juices.

"Shit," he groaned, gripping my ass cheek and giving it a little smack.

Pressing into me, he forced a moan to burst through my lips as he held it there. My pussy throbbed around his pole, and I shuddered shortly after as I came yet again. Teflon seemed to know my body better than I obviously did, because the smallest actions had me creaming uncontrollably.

"Ahhh, ahhh, ahh," I whined as he pounded me so hard I could barely make a complete sound.

Listening to him groan as he slammed me hard and fast, was enough for me to reach my peak yet again. Grasping the sheets in my hands, I clenched my teeth as his thick dick slammed my middle repeatedly, just before he spilled everything from inside of him, into me.

"Fuck, Tati," he exhaled before sliding out of me slowly.

I just laid there, still bent over for a moment until I finally gained some composure. By the time I stood up, Teflon had returned with a warm wet towel for me and for him. Once we were clean, we washed our hands.

"Stay inside until you have to go to that meeting Tatiana. I told you until I get that nigga, which will be soon I promise, I can't have you out on the town."

"Fine, fine," I rolled my eyes as he leaned down to kiss my lips.

I knew I was supposed to stay inside, but I really had some errands to run. So once Teflon had been gone for about fifteen minutes, I quickly got dressed and rushed down to my car. After stopping by the bank, I drove to the grocery store because Teflon was missing a lot of the things I liked to snack on, and he didn't have much available for me to cook.

As I was walking down the aisle where the cookies were, someone tapped me on the shoulder. I inhaled sharply before turning around, because I hoped it wasn't one of Brevin's people. Teflon would go insane, and if I lived to see it, it would be hell. Turning around slowly, still gripping my basket handle, I saw it was that hoe Amanda, rubbing her big ass belly and looking like she was sad as hell.

"What?" I snapped.

"Hey I know we kind of got off on the wrong foot but—"

"Kind of? You fucked my man, got pregnant by him, and then tried to blackmail me just recently. We didn't *kind of* get off on a bad foot, boo, we did. Now what the fuck do you want?"

"Money, I need money. Brevin doesn't want anything to do with me and he's blocked my number. I don't make enough money to handle a lot of my bills because he stopped helping me with them, and now the baby is coming… it's just gonna be too much."

"I'm sorry let me make sure I understand you. You don't have any money, and the first person you thought to ask was me?" I chuckled because it was actually funny.

"No my mother and sister help but they can only do so much. But you, you have that guy you're dating *and* Brevin's money."

"And why the fuck would I help you, Amanda? Give me one good reason."

"Well for one because you're a woman and I'm sure you can sympathize with me. And secondly because I know you're a good person."

"Well you thought wrong. Now get out of my fucking face before I knock you upside the head with these cookies." I shook the bag of cookies I'd picked up to let her know I was armed with my weapon of choice already.

"If you don't help me, I'm gonna tell Brevin about you and that guy I saw! Don't think I won't do it! Brevin will protect me from him, so I don't have to worry about getting killed."

Stopping, I chuckled as I turned around to look at her.

"Unfortunately for you whack body, Brevin already knows. But even if he didn't, do you honestly believe he would protect you from my man? He won't even pick up the phone for you and you're carrying his baby. But thanks for letting me know you were about to snitch, I'll be sure to pass that message to my nigga."

"Tatiana!" she called after me but I threw my hand up.

I finished shopping, and after I loaded up the car, I checked my phone. I let out a sigh of relief to see I only had messages from Jadynn and Cecily, none from Teflon going off about me leaving home. I darted to Teflon's apartment after getting a banana milkshake from Rally's, and luckily, some pretty chipper white chick helped me with the groceries since she lived two doors down from him.

I made myself a quick lunch, and then passed out while watching some daytime TV.

****

A few hours later…

I woke up and checked the time on my iPhone. My meeting with Zeus was in an hour, so I got out of bed and quickly rushed to the bathroom to brush my teeth and take another shower. Once out, I put on some skinny tan slacks, a cream blouse, and cream sandal stilettos; my usual work attire.

I tied up my hair, and when I looked into the mirror I saw I had a bruise on my neck from when Brevin tried to rape me. That shit immediately pissed me off, and I knew before Teflon got rid of him, I had to get my revenge on my own for all the shit he'd done to me; namely killing our baby. Brevin was gonna wish he'd never even looked my way.

I spritzed some perfume on, and then grabbed my purse and left out to Zeus' restaurant. I made it there about 15 minutes later, and saw that I was five minutes early which was unacceptable. I usually preferred a good 15, but that nap I'd taken was unexpected. I needed to start scheduling in my pregnancy symptoms.

I got out of my car and walked up to the front of the restaurant, and when I peered inside I saw Zeus talking to someone dressed up in cooking attire, like maybe he was a chef being hired.

"Hi," I spoke lowly after knocking on the window and getting Zeus' attention.

He smiled widely upon seeing me, and then jogged towards the front to let me in. When I stepped foot inside, I was in complete awe at how beautiful the place was. Everything was white, and/or gold, including the booth tables. The flatware was gold too, which was something I'd never seen in a restaurant. Zeus had clearly put a lot of money into this place.

"Wow," I smiled as I slid into one of the booth tables that he'd gestured for me to sit at. "I love the atmosphere it's very, umm—"

"Very late 1700's France?" he grinned and I nodded wearing one as well.

"Yes actually. I think it may be all the gold. I like it, but don't you think having gold utensils can be a bit pricey?"

"Yeah but I have the money to spare."

"I don't mean to be frank, or to pry, but how do you have so much money? Enough to have your patrons eating off of gold?"

"I'm in stocks. I've invested a lot, and in return I've gotten a lot."

"Well that's nice." I looked down to dig into my briefcase. "So the party is in a month, and I'm gonna have the people who have to set up come in five days before the date, just in case something needs to be redone or ordered, we will have time."

"Sounds good to me."

"Great. I just need you to sign this contract here, which basically states that you agree for journalists, food critics, and photographers to come work, and that they will receive free food."

"Absolutely." He took the documents, and began to scribble on them.

"Great." I surveyed the documents once he was done. "So do you have any questions?"

"No I don't— well I have one. I was wondering if you'd stay with me for a little while and taste some of the food. I'm hiring a chef and I want someone to taste test with me."

"Uh, sure yeah I guess I can do that. I can't stay too long though."

"All I need is an hour, maybe less."

"Okay."

Zeus went to the back to I guess get the chef, and while he was gone, I went into my texts to message Jadynn.

Me: Hey, I'm gonna be tasting the food for Zeus' restaurant. If Teflon asks, just say I'm working because that's what I'm gonna say.

Jadynn: Hmm, is there a reason why we're lying?

Me: It's not lying. I'm actually working.

Jadynn: I don't remember tasting food being part of the job, but I got you.

Me: Thanks!

As soon as I put my phone up, Zeus was returning with two glasses of wine, and a chef following behind him carrying a few plates of food.

"This is gonna be the best wine you've ever tasted," Zeus smiled as he set the glass in front of me, and slid into the booth.

"Hello, Miss Drew, I'm Chef Cellini," the cook shook my hand and then proceeded to introduce the dishes.

I only took a very small sip of the wine because I was with child. I didn't want Zeus all in my business because that just wasn't something he needed to know.

After I was finished helping him with this restaurant, he would be passed over to another one of Eddie's associates and I would never talk to him again. That's just how shit worked.

"I think I like everything," I dabbed my mouth with the cloth napkin after tasting the last dish.

"I can tell, but yes I agree. Cellini is great. You know, you should really stay and try his—"

"Mr. Rydell I have to go."

He stared at me for a moment and then said, "Right yes of course."

"So I'll be calling you soon."

As I got out of the booth, he quickly got down to help me out. He guided me out of the restaurant, and when I felt his hand on my lower back, I moved away.

"Have a nice night beautiful."

"Goodnight, Mr. Rydell."

I climbed into my car, and then blasted the heat because I was so damn cold. It was nighttime and getting to be fall, so the air was much brisker. As I drove towards Teflon's apartment, Brevin crossed my mind and how much I hated him. I made a detour and drove to the home I used to live in, and then parked across the street. I sat there for a moment, wondering what I was going to do, and then when I remembered I had crowbar in my trunk, I hopped out and retrieved it.

Walking across the street and up to the garage, I used the remote I still had, for the door to lift. When my eyes landed on Brevin's precious Porsche 911, a smile crept across my face.

CRASH!

I whacked the back window, and the adrenaline that pumped through me was invigorating almost. I continued to burst out his windows, ignoring the loud ass alarm going off. As I dragged the edge of the crowbar around the car, leaving deep gashes and scratches, Brevin came stumbling into the garage wearing only his boxers and his slippers. He looked dazed and confused, and his face was still messed up from when Teflon fucked him up.

"Tati are you fucking serious!" he screeched, hands repeatedly moving up and down from his head to his waistline as he took in the damage.

I ignored him, beating on the hood of the car, and messing up the once pristine silver paint.

"Tatiana I'm gonna fucking kill—"

WHAM!

I whacked him across the face with the crowbar, and he fell back into the shelf, causing a bunch of shit to collapse down onto him. Once the things stop cascading from the shelf, I continued to hit him with the crowbar as he screamed and tried to reach for it. I beat him until I was tired and until I heard him crying for the first time ever.

Standing up straight, I panted heavily as I stared down at him, sobbing like a bitch and already bruising. It wasn't enough to make me forget about the baby he'd made me lose, but it would do for now.

"Ah!" he yelped when I stabbed him in the side with my heel.

Grabbing a handful of his curly hair, I yanked his head back and leaned down into his face to say, "Tell me you're a punk bitch."

"Fuck y-you!" he shivered. I grasped his hair tighter, forcing him to wince in pain, and then grabbed the crowbar back up to hit him but he stopped me. "Aight Tati! I'm a bitch!"

"A punk bitch I said!"

"A punk bitch, baby just put the fucking—"

"I'm not your baby!"

"Tatiana, please put the crow bar down," he sniffled, blood seeping from his lip since I'd went across his face earlier. The sight of my little ass overpowering him was probably hilarious.

I finally let his hair go, and then walked around the right side of the car, since he was blocking the left. As I left the garage, I hit the button so that the door could come back down. I then climbed into my vehicle, and went home to Teflon to sleep like a baby.

That shit felt way too good.

CHAPTER SIXTEEN

Teflon

I felt Tatiana get into the bed after she was in the shower for fucking ever. The scent of her soap hit me hard, as she got comfortable in my bed, and then laid down. Turning over, I gripped her small frame from behind, making her jump slightly.

"How the fuck you getting home later than me?" I quizzed, kissing her neck and letting my hands caress her thigh.

"When I first get a client, I always have to work pretty late. There is a lot to do and stuff."

"Who is this client again?"

"Uh, just this boring stock guy. He's opening a restaurant now, and he hired us to do PR for it and him."

"Dope. I always wanted to own a restaurant."

She looked over her shoulder at me and said, "Really?"

"Yeah. I'm gonna do that shit too. If you ain't know, I'm gonna be coming into a lot more money soon," I smiled and so did she.

"Well I can't wait to see what you come up with. I can help you,

you know?"

"Of course. Why you think I'm telling you?" I hugged her body tighter, and slipped my hand under her gown to caress her stomach. "I'm hoping that if I break yo' sexy ass off I can get some free services."

"We'll just have to see about that."

I cupped her face, and then turned it towards me so I could kiss her lips a few times. Her eyes darted all over my face, before a warm smile crept across it. I pecked her once more, and then we both readjusted to get comfortable enough to sleep.

***

The next night…

I walked into my mother's place, looking around for everybody because it was so damn quiet. As I moved further to the back, I could hear my mom having a phone conversation. I knocked lightly and came in, and when she saw me her face lit up.

"Chi, let me call you back okay? My boy is here and he rarely comes," she grinned at me and I just shook my head at her.

"Ma you don't have to get off now." I knew Chi was one of her good friends from Vietnam. She didn't talk to her much, and because of that my mother was rather lonely, especially when my father disappeared.

"It's fine." She said to me but nodded to whatever Chi was saying as if she could see her. Finally she hung up, and walked around her bed to hug me with her short self. "I never expected you to come at this time."

"I know but I was over here, and I came because I needed to ask you something. I want you to meet Tatiana, and I was thinking that maybe this weekend would be cool."

"Yes that's okay. " She walked into the kitchen and I followed her to sit at the table. "What does she like to eat?"

"You can make whatever, or we can just go to dinner or something," I replied and she nodded. "So where is Thomas?"

"He and Cameron went to the movies."

"I can't keep up with his ass— I mean him. And now with Torrey getting out in two weeks, I feel like I'm gonna have to keep an eye on them both. But ain't nobody got time to be looking out for Torrey. Nigga is older than me."

"I know, but you know his brain hasn't matured like yours. I've always told you in reality, you're the oldest and Torrey is the youngest," she smiled as she started some tea.

I was about to speak but the sound of tires screeching down the street and then about seven loud gunshots cut me off. My mom didn't live in the best neighborhood, but there weren't shootouts like this happening all the time, if at all.

"Get down!" I yelled to my mother, who dropped to the floor.

I reached for my gun and slowly made it to the front to look through the window. My eyes scanned as much of the street as I could see, and that's when I recognized my mother's car in the middle of it. I frowned, because I didn't get why her car would have been the one making all that fucking noise… but that's when it hit me, and my heart dropped.

"No, no fuck no." I yanked the front door open and ran like I was Forrest Gump to her car.

When I got to it, my body became weak as hell seeing my little brother slumped up against the wheel in the front seat, and his girlfriend Cameron in the passenger side screaming. Feeling tears well up, I yanked the driver's side door open to look at my brother.

"Thomas, Thomas man get up!" I knew he was dead but I continued to plead, smacking his face lightly hoping it would revive his ass some how. "Get up!!!" I screamed to him again, before looking to a shaken up Cameron. "What the fuck happened!"

"I-I don't know! They… they followed us and—"

"Teflon!" I heard my mother yell from her front door.

"Ma go back inside!" I looked over my shoulder to see her approaching.

"What is going…" She stopped talking once she recognized Thomas lying on the steering wheel lifeless. "No! No! Not my baby! Call somebody so we can save him!" she shouted, dropping to the ground and tugging on Thomas' shirt.

"Ma— Ma he's gone! Go back in the house. And Cameron, tell me what happened please?" I tried to stay calm, and talk calmer so that I wouldn't cry like some hoe.

"They followed us and he…" She sniffled, breathing hard.

"Cam get out the car."

"No I can't leave him he's—"

"He's dead! Get out the damn car!"

She slowly unbuckled her seat belt, and started to shake her head repeatedly as she climbed out of the car. She came around, and I looked her over to make sure she was alright. I then nodded towards the house, and she went inside like my mom had.

I stood there surveying my brother, not even caring if the niggas came back and got me. This shit was not supposed to happen to him. He was the good nigga, the muthafucka that made it out and did something with his life, yet he was lying here in this car, dead just like he was some hoodlum who had his hand deep off in some shit.

"Fuck!" I shouted in the street, gripping my hair and closing my eyes so tears wouldn't come down.

Suddenly I heard the ambulance in the distance, and when I looked to the front door of my mother's home, she had the phone clutched in her hand, crying.

The ambulance finally made it to my mom's street, and they hopped out with the quickness to approach the car.

"He's dead," I mumbled.

"What happened? Did he just die—"

"He died instantly," I spoke lowly as fuck, voice cracking a little bit as I watched them pull his lifeless body from the car. He had two shots to his head, one on his neck, and another in his shoulder.

They placed Thomas in this black bag on the stretcher, and before they could zip it up, my mom came running out, trying to touch him. I had to grab her after a little while so they could take him away.

The police questioned my mother and me for a moment, then

they asked Cameron some questions. All she knew was that they followed my bother, and he didn't notice until it was too late and they'd started shooting. They got him in the shoulder but he kept driving, and when he turned on the street they blew his fucking… I have to take a deep breath. They blew his fucking head open and then shot him in the neck.

I stayed at my mom's house until about 2am, because that was when Cameron and her finally fell asleep. Tatiana was blowing my phone up for obvious reasons, but I just didn't feel like talking. As I drove to my spot, I kept replaying what Cameron told the police in my mind. It was like they were purposely aiming for my brother. Thomas wasn't into shit like that, and the last fight his ass got into was probably when he was a freshman in high school.

My mind raced constantly trying to think of who was behind this bullshit, so much so that I almost ran a red light. As I sat there, it all came to me; it was that nigga Brevin.

Running the red light anyway, I made a U-turn, headed towards Brevin's spot in Ohio City. I was done planning on this nigga. He'd gone too far murking my brother and I knew it was his ass. Like I said, Thomas didn't have enemies, and Torrey had been in jail too damn long to have any left. Not to mention, why would any enemies of Torrey's choose *now* to retaliate for anything? Nah this was Brevin's muthafucking ass and he was gonna meet his maker tonight.

I parked all fucked up when I made it to his crib, slipped on my black gloves, and walked right up to the front door. I took one of them big ass potted plants, and tossed it through the front, sending off the alarm. I didn't give a fuck though. Hopping into the window, I booked it upstairs like a champion track runner, and burst off into his room to see him laid up with that bitch who was pregnant by him and tried to press Tatiana in the bathroom.

WHAM!

I whacked his ass across the face, waking him up, and when he saw me he quickly sat up, and so did the girl, covering her naked body.

"My brother nigga?" I laughed angrily, gripping my gun tightly.

Brevin just stared up at me emotionless for a few moments, before a smug grin covered his face.

"Yeah I got at yo' goodie two shoes ass brother you bitch ass nigga—"

PHEW! PHEW! PHEW! PHEW!

"Ahhhhh!" Amanda hollered.

PHEW!

The first shot I sent through Brevin's head killed him, but I had to give him three more just because, and then I killed his bitch for screaming. I hightailed it out of there, and once I got to my car I sped off on two wheels, knowing the police would be here soon since the alarm had been going off. I did about 90mph all the way to my crib, and once I parked I shut the engine off and took a few deep breaths.

I tried, I really did, but eventually I just broke down and cried like a fucking newborn for my brother.

CHAPTER SEVENTEEN

Merce

One week later…

$\mathcal{I}$ sat next to Teflon, as his mother, Groove, my brother Sebastian, Thomas' girlfriend Cameron, and I rode in the limo so we could go see the body be put into the ground at Eerie Street Cemetery. I'd known Thomas since he was a little ass baby in diapers, and I couldn't believe that Brevin had taken his life. He didn't deserve that shit, but in the game nobody was off limits, not even a harmless college boy who'd worked hard in order to have nothing to do with that shit.

I wanted to be mad at Teflon for going against the plan yet again and killing Brevin without thinking, but like the last time I couldn't blame him. Brevin somehow figured out just how to hurt Teflon as badly as he'd hurt him by taking Tatiana. This shit was fucking with me, because Teflon and I both were to blame for this shit happening, and I would have to live with that for the rest of my life. And even though I know we all wanted to go sit in dark corners and cry for a moment, we had to keep moving and do hella damage control in order to take over Brevin's shit, without facing repercussions from murking his ass too early.

After surrounding the body and listening to the preacher say a few words, all of us returned to the limo and went to back to the Church of God in Christ for the repast. They were right across the street from one another so we could have walked, but as a funeral tradition, we took the limo and had it drive us through the cemetery and then back out to the church.

I spotted Jadynn outside wearing a black dress, and she was standing next to Tatiana and Cecily who were wearing the same. I hugged them all, and then draped my arm around Jadynn as we entered the church.

"You okay?" She rubbed my back.

"Nope."

She and Tatiana knew someone had broken into Brevin's home and murdered him and that Amanda bitch, but no one knew who it was. I just knew that Teflon had left some evidence behind because he was so reckless with it, but I guess since he literally went in and out, he didn't leave much behind for them to work with.

We all got our plates, and sat at the table with Teflon's mother, Tam, as people kept coming up to her to express their gratitude.

"Aye let her fucking eat in peace!" Teflon barked, eventually getting tired of the people bothering his mother.

"Mrs. German, I'm sorry that this is the first time we've met, and it's under these circumstances," Tatiana touched Tam's hand.

"Especially because this is all your fault," Tam replied, catching us all off guard as she snatched her hand from Tatiana.

"What?" Tatiana frowned.

"Ma what are you taking about?" Teflon added.

"If you would have never been trying to take her from that lunatic he wouldn't have done this to my baby. She's not even worth it!" Tam screamed, Vietnamese accent pungent as fuck.

"Excuse me." Tatiana scooted her chair back and got up from the table.

"Ma, you're extra as fuck right now."

"Tre'Wayne, your mouth you—"

"Nah this don't have nothing to do with her! I chose to work for that nigga, and I chose to pursue her. You acting like she came and seduced me or some shit out of nowhere. I started this shit with Brevin and that's it! It don't have shit to do with her like I said!" Teflon got up from the table and went after Tatiana.

No words were exchanged as the rest of us sat at the table and finished eating. After a while, Jadynn, Sebastian, and I left, saying our goodbyes to Tam and Cameron, since Groove and Cecily were leaving as well.

"Hey so we need to meet up tonight," Groove stopped me once we got by my car.

"I know." I nodded, holding the door open for Jadynn. "I know."

Later that night…

"Leaving already?" Jadynn quizzed, lying in my bed with the covers pulled up to cover her naked body.

"Yeah, shouldn't take me too long. Just a little meeting." I pulled my hood over my head and leaned down to kiss her soft ass lips. Her reddish brown hair was a bit disheveled, but I found that shit to be hella sexy.

"Okay," she whispered softly before I left the bedroom and bumped right into Sebastian.

"Damn nigga, take yo' ass to bed or some shit. You better not had been listening to us fuck, Bash." I moved around him and he followed me.

"Nah not even. But aye you should let me come along with you to whatever meeting you got. I wanna be in this shit Mer—"

"Did you not go to a funeral for Thomas today?" I frowned, staring down at him.

"Yeah but—"

"Then what the fuck would make you think that I would purposely bring you into this shit huh? I told you to find some work, and when I said that I meant some legal shit."

"So it's okay for you to hustle but not me?"

"Hustling ain't just about selling drugs or doing shit that could get you locked up stupid! Hustling is making sure you get your money, and that can include working multiple jobs, which are legal. Find some shit, enroll in school, or get the fuck out," I hissed, and he just stared up at me frowning before turning to walk back to his bedroom. "Stupid muthafucka," I mumbled as I snatched my keys off the counter.

If Sebastian wanted part of this drug bullshit, he couldn't stay with me. He had to get his ass on and do his own shit. I'll be damned if I'm at his funeral because I let him join me in this shit. I know my parents would blame for it too, and for the first time I wouldn't be able to say or do anything about their mouths.

When I got down to my car, and was about to pull the door open, a familiar whip sped past me. I realized it was Savannah's car, and exhaled heavily. I'd totally forgotten about her fucking threats in the midst of all this shit I was dealing with. I didn't need this right now, I really didn't.

Hopping into my whip, I sped to this warehouse that Teflon had recently found when we were still playing Brevin for a fool. As soon as shut my engine off, my phone rang and I looked to see it was Mack calling me through the burner app. Nigga didn't have my real number and it was for good reasoning.

"What?" I answered, angrily.

"Hey umm, I had time to think and I'm down."

"Why now? You took forever, and now all of a sudden you're trying to be down? Shit sounds fishy to me," I chuckled.

Nigga wasn't thinking about me until Brevin's ass got murked. I knew that was the only reason he was agreeing because for one, come on, I'd have to be stupid to think otherwise, and two, I could hear the desperation in his voice. Bitch ass nigga was too scared to even think about running shit on his own. Mack was smart as fuck, but he was one of those niggas that performed best in the background. He liked to be the director, while letting other people act.

"Nah I knew I wanted to rock with y'all from the time you came to see me, but I just needed time to think."

"Aight well, I'll send you an address and I need you to come in the next fifteen minutes."

"Yeah yeah, that's fine."

I hung up with him and got out of the car to approach Teflon and Groove who were sitting a little bit away. I dapped them both up, and then sat down in one of the empty chairs.

"I'm trying to figure out how we can get his team. We ain't even have a chance to eliminate who needs to be eliminated. I know that shit is my fault, but I had to what I had to do for my brother," Teflon scratched his head. "You ain't got no pull with any of 'em?" he looked to Groove.

"I do, well did, but I'm yo' cousin nigga so they ain't gonna fuck with me like that."

"We need someone who was close to Brevin to convince them niggas. Somebody like Mack, and he's gon' be here in a little bit," I smiled, and soon enough Teflon and Groove were wearing the same expressions.

I had a feeling this would be like taking candy from a baby. So why did I also feel like danger was lurking?

CHAPTER EIGHTEEN

Ryan "Groove" Barten

The next day...

$\mathcal{I}$ let the shower water rinse the soap from my body, and get all in my face. I was tired already and shit, the day hadn't even started. Cutting the water off, I stepped out and grabbed a towel to wrap around my waist. Entering my bedroom, I saw Cecily putting her earrings in, while looking at me through the mirror.

"Where is Rye?" I quizzed, referring to my son.

"In the kitchen eating his cereal," she sighed. "I was thinking that maybe tonight we could all go eat or do something together."

"I would love to baby, but I can't at the moment." I pulled some boxers from the drawer as I spoke, and I could see her frustration out the corner of my eye.

"Let me guess, you have to work," she spat, storming past me and snatching her t-shirt up off the bed.

"Nah actually, I umm... just have something to do."

"You have something to do, even though Brevin is gone." I didn't respond, so she said, "And you stopped working with him before that! So what's up?"

"All I'm saying is that I have something to do."

She moved closer to me and hugged me from behind as I zipped my jeans.

"Please have lunch with us. We can go right after Rye gets out of preschool, and then I will let you go for the rest of the day."

"Cecily, I can't."

"Of course." She let me go, slipped her feet into her shoes, and then walked out of the bedroom calling my son's name.

I hated to treat my girl like this but I had no choice right now. The universe seemed to be working against my ass, and until I get shit straight, Cecily would just have to ride this shit out with me. We'd been together for forever, and I'd always made her my priority, so in my eyes she could fall back for a little bit and come second temporarily.

After I put on my t-shirt, wristwatch, chain, and shoes, I put lotion on my hands and then a little bit of cologne. I unlocked the drawer that I kept my phone in overnight, and hit the home button to see if I had any notifications.

Yeah I said I kept my shit locked up and it was because Cecily liked to go through it. Last time I almost slapped the shit out of her, so to prevent that I locked it up. I didn't need her ass in my business like that, because she'd try to use it to run me and I wasn't with that.

As I looked at my phone, I sighed because like always the shit was blown the fuck up. Pocketing it, I left the bedroom and then my crib after kissing my son goodbye.

Pulling onto West 48th over in Clark-Fulton, I came to a stop when I reached my destination. Getting out, I went into the backseat to get the Target bags I'd brought over here and then headed up the walkway. I knocked lowly, and then waited until Anya opened the door, holding my six-month-old daughter Brin.

Anya was this girl I started fucking with about two years ago, and it unexpectedly turned into some more shit. I planned to just smash and move on, but not only was the pussy good, her personality was addictive. She knew I had a girl from day one, but like me she just couldn't end the relationship so we kept it going. One thing eventually led to another, and another, and then my daughter Brin was conceived.

There was no way I was gonna tell Cecily about Brin because Cecily wasn't like them other hoes you know, that would leave me for two weeks and then take me back because she loved me. Nah Cecily would never talk to my ass again, even though we had a son together. We'd be co-parenting on mute.

Thankfully Anya was compliant with my wishes to keep this shit a secret, so everything had been cool between us, especially since I was doing my part with Brin. And Anya wasn't some hood rat bitch that slept around or acted a fool when I didn't text back. She had a college degree and a good job at Cleveland Vehicle Detention. And to be honest, I didn't know who I wanted to be with, but I knew I didn't want to lose either. I guess you could say I was in two relationships, and between trying to overthrow Brevin, and being a man in two families basically, I barely had time to myself.

"Say hi daddy," Anya smiled, moving Brin's chunky arm up and down as she cooed and smiled up at me.

Anya was sexy as hell with her supple caramel skin, and slim thick frame. She kept her hair short like Nia Long's in *Friday*, and even though I didn't like short hair, hers worked well with her sexy ass face. She and Cecily looked different in the sense that Cecily was thick through and through. She didn't have a flat stomach like Anya, and she had a bigger butt and bigger tits. It was like the best of both worlds having them two.

I grinned at my beautiful baby girl, and entered the home to set all the shit down that I'd bought. Taking Brin from Anya, I kissed Anya on the lips before sitting down with my daughter. I pecked her cheeks a few times as she shoved her hand into her own mouth.

"She has a doctor's appointment coming up, so do you think you'll be able to make it?" Anya inquired, watching me play with Brin.

"Of course."

"I have to ask, Ryan; how long is this gonna go on? I mean this isn't me, being some side chick and I don't want to—"

"You ain't a fucking side chick and I told you to stop saying that."

"How am I not? You live with her, she doesn't know about me, but I know about her, Ryan! That's exactly what a side chick is and I don't wanna be that anymore. I'm tired of it."

"So what are you saying, Anya? Say what the fuck you really mean so we can get this conversation over with."

"I want you to make a choice to either be with me, or to be with her. Of course I won't stop letting you see Brin if you choose her, but I can't continue this. It's not me and I have a lot going for myself."

I just stared at Anya for a moment, trying to think of way out of this damn conversation. I didn't want to choose right now because I couldn't. I had longevity with Cecily and she was my girl, the one everyone expected me to be with forever and marry; she deserved that shit too. But I knew there was no way I could leave Anya alone forever either.

"Look I love you Anya and I don't wanna lose you."

"But?"

"But nothing. That's it. I love you, my daughter, and what I know we can build together. So I'm gonna see where you and I can go."

"For real?" she smiled widely.

"Yeah for real."

"Does that mean you're gonna sleep here tonight then?" She folded her arms, raising her eyebrow.

"Yeah. After I handle some business, I'll be home."

I didn't know how I was gonna pull this shit off, but like always I'd figure it out eventually.

CHAPTER NINETEEN

Jadynn

"Today was great, Jadynn," Dr. Larney, my therapist smiled. "I think you're getting much better honey. You're so different from the last few sessions we've had."

"I feel different."

"And why do you think that is?" She closed up her notepad. I didn't know if there was an answer I was supposed to give, or if she wanted what I really thought.

"Well I haven't been in contact with my mother, sister, or ex boyfriend lately, and I guess keeping myself away from them has been helping."

"I see. Well it's okay for now, but don't keep that up. Hiding is not going to solve anything. You need to face your fears, not run away from them."

"Got it," I nodded, half smiling. I had no plans on facing my fears any time soon, but maybe somewhere in the far future.

I scheduled to come back in a week, and then I left the office.

I wanted to get some Starbucks for breakfast before I went to work, so I stopped at the Starbucks on 6th Street because I wanted to eat outside and enjoy how nice of a day it was.

After I picked up my iced tea and breakfast sandwich, I went to sit down outside, liking the way the sun beamed on me. As I watched some guy unhook his bike from the rack, something big and tall blocked my vision. Looking up, I saw it was Russell and immediately reached for my pepper spray.

"Relax, Jadynn, I just want to talk," he threw his hands up and sat down across from me. The only reason I hadn't sprayed him yet was because 6th street was pretty busy around this time, and he'd be a fool to try anything.

"I don't have shit to say to you and you shouldn't have any fucking thing to say to me either."

"I know you hate me and I even hate myself for all the shit I've done to you. From messing around with Paige, to you know… breaking into your apartment and umm…"

"Raping me?"

"Yeah." His eyes bounced around my face for a moment before he said, "I'm sorry for all of that and I want—"

"Russell why are you here? How did you even find me?"

"I followed you from your apartment this morning, to what looked like some doctor's building. You aight? Everything good?"

"Look, leave me the fuck alone. Don't worry about me. Don't think about me, and don't ever follow me again or something worse than that ass beating you got will happen."

"Man, he caught me off guard."

"Right."

"Jadynn, I'm here because I love you and I know you still love me..." his voice trailed off when I started to laugh loudly. "What's funny?"

"The fact that you think I'm in love with you! I didn't want your ass when I had you!"

"So why the fuck did you give me hell about fucking around with Paige if you didn't want me huh?"

"I was upset because of the betrayal nigga, not because I felt like she'd taken the love of my life or something. Please! She did me a favor by taking yo' leeching ass because I found something way better."

"I just want another chance, baby. I got a job working at UPS, and I'm doing well. I'm getting my shit together like you always wanted."

"What about your unborn with my sister?"

"I mean I'm still gon' handle my business, but we ain't gotta be together." He sucked his teeth when I laughed again. "Jadynn, stop treating me like this baby."

"Wait so let me get this shit straight. You were a good for nothing ass nigga when I had you, couldn't even pay a bill if your life depended on it, then *you* have the nerve to cheat with my sister, and then proceed to rape me after that, yet you thought following me around town and giving me a sorry ass apology was gonna make me take you back?"

"Stop making it seem like you were fucking perfect! All you did was work, and chill with Tatiana and that fat bitch!"

"Yeah that was all I did, you're right. And that's what I'm still doing and my man now doesn't have a problem with it you know why? Because he has his own business that has to tend to. He's not sitting up in front of the TV with a beer and box of Ritz Crackers, crying because his woman is out making money."

"Watch yo' fucking mou— ahhhh!" he screeched when I sprayed his ass with my pepper spray. I damn near emptied the fucking bottle on his ass.

"No you watch your mouth nigga!" I hissed, standing up and shoving my spray back into my purse. I quickly snatched up my food, feeling all eyes on me as I stormed off to my car.

I drove to work and just ate my food in the car before going up. I knew today would be busy, so eating at my desk would mean cold food. I didn't need shit else ruining my day after Russell popping up.

I reached in the back to grab my purse, and then when I opened the door to get out my car, another vehicle flew by me going like 100mph, almost knocking my damn door off the hinges. I had to pause for a moment and thank God I hadn't stepped out yet, as I watched the car hook a quick right.

"What the fuck?" I mumbled, frowning as I got out and went up inside of the building I worked in.

I took the elevator up to my floor, and when I walked passed Tatiana's glass office, I entered and sat down as she finished up a phone call.

"Was that your new boo?" I chuckled as she rolled her eyes and hung up the phone.

"I don't have a new boo, and shut your mouth."

"So did he express his love to you over drinks and food?"

"No he did not, because that's unprofessional. He's a client and nothing else. And stop talking so loudly."

"Teflon's not here."

"That's what he wants us to think," she replied, making us both laugh.

"I saw Russell today, and before you say anything let me finish. He followed me from my apartment, waited outside while I had my therapy session, and then decided to approach me while I was eating at the Starbucks on 6th."

"To say what?" Tatiana's eyes were wide, and her lips were slightly parted.

"That he wanted me back basically."

"No."

"Yes. I was so damn offended that he even thought I would even think about taking his raggedy ass back. He's lucky I didn't press charges on his ass for what he did."

"Why don't you?"

"You know why, Tati."

"Yeah but why not make him pay? I mean yeah Merce beat his ass and got his revenge, but what about yours?"

She raised her brow and I just stared at her, pondering. I didn't want to go through all that, but I admit not getting my own personal revenge on Russell did bother me some.

CHAPTER TWENTY

Tatiana

I swayed my hips to the music playing from my phone as I put some curl cream into my hair. Today I was off, and I had already started my get myself together routine. Whenever I got super swamped with work, a lot of my body maintenance suffered, like shaving, washing my hair, and getting my nails done. So today, I was taking care of all of that, as long as this baby growing inside of me would allow it.

As I stared at myself in the mirror, a smile spread across my face. I couldn't help but to be happy about my life in it's current state. I had a good job, and even better man, and I was finally gonna be a mother. Not to mention, Brevin was out of my life and forever. Teflon came clean to me about being the culprit, and I threw this pussy his way as a thank you gift to his surprise.

I will admit that some nights I'm still afraid that one of Brevin's people will fuck me up, or that he's not really dead, but I'm slowly getting over that. Teflon said he had it all under control, and since he hasn't steered me wrong yet, I'm gonna continue to believe him.

Another thing bothering me was the fact that Teflon's mother didn't like me and blamed me for the murder of her youngest. What was worse though, was the fact that I could understand how she came to such a horrible conclusion. Had I not come into Teflon's life, Thomas would be alive.

Speaking of Teflon, he'd left early today, but he left me a note promising that he would take me somewhere tonight; anywhere of my choice. It was the little things like that, that made me love him. He wasn't like Brevin who was only nice to get me, and then an asshole once he had me, but that was because Teflon actually loved me and Brevin just wanted to own me.

I attempted to turn my music off once I had on my bra and panties, and as soon as I did, my phone rang. I didn't mean to answer since the number looked strange, but because I was trying to turn off my Pandora station, I accidentally answered anyway.

"Hello?" I rolled my eyes, not caring who it was. I wasn't in the mood for anybody or anything that wasn't Teflon or Jadynn.

"Tatiana!" Brevin's mother screeched into the phone.

"Mrs. Williamson." I turned the phone off of speakerphone and put it to my ear as I left the bathroom and entered the bedroom.

"Hi honey, I've been looking all over for you."

"Oh I've been busy you know, trying to keep my mind off of everything."

"Yes I understand. Well Breeze and I are going to pick out some funeral arrangements this evening and we want you to come along. I mean it's only right."

Breeze? When did she get to Ohio?

"I well—"

"Please, Tatiana, we need to do this together for Brevin."

"Yeah sure. Okay," I sighed.

"Great so meet us at my house at noon. We'll go to pick out the casket and then maybe after I can cook us some lunch."

"Sounds like a plan, Mrs. Williamson."

I was having a good ass day, and now she just had to ruin the shit.

I looked at the clock and saw it was 10am, so since I had some time I went ahead and made myself some breakfast. And with the way this baby had me feeling… I needed a feast.

As I scarfed down the pancakes, sausage, bacon, egg scramble, and English muffin with orange juice, my phone started to ring. I saw it was Eddie, and even though he was my boss I decided to answer. My job was different in that he couldn't ask me to come into work or anything, so if he was calling it must have been an emergency or problem.

"Hello?"

"Tatiana, you have a delivery down here at work."

I swallowed my juice and then reached for my planner to look through it and see if I'd mistakenly scheduled a delivery and forgot due to pregnancy brain.

"A delivery? I didn't schedule anything."

"It's a personal delivery I'm pretty sure. Can you come and get it today? I can have one of the drivers help you take it home."

"Eddie I'm not feeling too well. Uh, can't they just bring it to me?"

"Yeah sure."

"But I will text you the address. I'm not at my usual home anymore."

"Okay great. Enjoy your day off sweetie."

"Thanks."

I quickly shot Eddie a text with Teflon's address, and paced back and forth wondering what personal delivery could have come for me. I gave up and finished eating, and about 20 minutes into me watching TV, I got a call from one of the driver's named Tony saying he was downstairs. I quickly slipped some shoes on, and then went down to meet him at his truck.

"So what is it?" I questioned him as he hopped out the delivery like truck with Eddie's company name on it.

"Someone is very fond of you," Tony chuckled as he led me around the back of the truck.

He lifted the sliding door, and my jaw dropped at the four cases of roses. There were about one hundred red roses in each white round case, and they were beautiful.

"Did you read the card?" I inquired, taking the white card from one of them.

"Nope."

Just something to let you know I'm thinking of you. - Zeus

"Shit. Can you drive these to the garbage somewhere? I can't take these up inside, Tony. My boyfriend is going to flip if he sees them."

"Tell him they're from a girlfriend."

"He knows all my friends." I looked around the lot, then reached into my pocket for a $50. "Here, just to toss all of this."

"Thanks." He took it. "But I will just take these home to my wife. The instruction card here says they last for a year."

"Sure whatever; just take them."

Tony nodded and I turned around and headed back up inside. I grabbed my purse because it was almost time to go meet Brevin's mother and sister, and while on my way to my car I dialed Eddie.

"Hello honey!" Eddie sang with his flamboyant ass.

"Eddie, we have a problem."

"With?"

"That big client Zeus he's—"

"No no no, Tatiana Drew. Zeus is one of the biggest clients we've had this month. I don't care if he asks you to ride a donkey to work instead of driving… you do it. Once we finish his party, you will never even work with him again; Elle will. So just take whatever temporary hit."

"He sent me four cases of one hundred roses, Eddie. He wants more than PR services." I snatched my car door open, threw my purse in, and then hopped into the driver's side.

"Just bat your eyelashes, smile, say thank you, and steer him back to the subject at hand. Tatiana this isn't the first time a male client has been interested in you, so why are you so shaken up about this one?"

"I'm not!"

"Then why are we on the phone?" he giggled as I rolled my eyes. "I mean you can say it, we all think it. Zeus is a very sexy man."

"Well I have a man of my own, one who wouldn't be too fond of me receiving roses from another."

"Tati, just keep it professional like you've done it the past, get the job done, and move on to the next new client we get. Brevin will never know."

I was caught off guard when he mentioned Brevin, but then I had to remember that most people assumed I was still with him.

"Brevin passed, Eddie."

"Oh well... Wow I'm sorry to hear that. Who is— what boyfriend are you speaking of?"

"Brevin and I broke up before he died and I met someone else. But yeah I will just umm, try to keep Zeus' mind on the business."

"Great. And again, I'm sorry for your loss. I will have to meet this new guy though."

"Yep. Bye."

As soon as I hung up, Brevin's mother was calling. I told her I was on my way, and after talking my ear off *still,* she finally let me go. I made it to her home about 10 minutes later, and she and Breeze were already standing outside waiting on the porch.

Fuck...

"Hey ladies," I smiled, stepping onto the sidewalk as we approached one another and hugged.

As usual Breeze was standoffish. She moved down to Kentucky

with her boyfriend, and after she left she never looked back. She and Brevin never talked, and I was surprised to even see her here to help with his funeral.

"You look well, Tati." Mrs. Williamson hugged me tightly. We used to be close until I met Teflon.

"Thanks. Same to you."

"A little too well," Breeze mumbled.

"Excuse me?" I quizzed nicely. She just shook her head and smiled as we walked to her Kia truck and got in.

Mrs. Williamson talked the whole ride to the casket place, letting us know everything that she'd gotten in order. It was annoying as hell, but I felt bad for even being irritated. Her son was killed, and I knew all too well how badly it hurt to lose a child. I could only imagine how much worse it would be if I'd raised the child and actually got to know their personality like she'd done with Brevin. But did I regret him dying? No, because it was either me or him, and well...

We spent three fucking hours at the funeral home, and I'd peed so many times that Mrs. Williamson and Breeze were giving me the side eye. They were both women, and had both had babies, so they knew the signs. Not to mention I was already starving again, and snacking on the Teddy Grahams in my purse.

Once Mrs. Williamson picked a casket, we decided to go have some lunch at this Italian place Downtown named Chinato.

"So how are you holding up, Tati?" Mrs. Williamson asked as I scanned the menu, wanting everything on it.

"I'm gr— I don't really know how to feel," I caught myself. Almost said I was great; typical Freudian slip.

"You weren't home when any of it happened?" Breeze raised a brow.

"Uh no I was out of town." I looked down to reach for my buzzing phone.

Teflon: Wyd? Send me something.

Me: Lol can't. Kind of busy.

Teflon: You supposed to be naked in a robe all day. Just open that shit and send me a flick.

Me: No nigga lol

"Tatiana," Mrs. Williamson got my attention. "I'm happy to see that your phone can make you smile so widely, considering the fact that something tragic has happened to the man you love."

"Mhm," I nodded, shoving some of the bread they'd brought to the table into my mouth.

"You just happened to be out of town, when Brevin get's murdered?" Breeze went right back to the conversation before.

"You know what no, I was with my new boyfriend, in the bed sleep," I said just before a waitress came to the table. She took our orders, and then I sat back in my chair, grabbing another piece of bread to bite as these two fools stared at me astonished.

"You were out with another man while my child was being killed?" Mrs. Williamson's lip trembled.

I'd said what I said because I was tired of pretending with these two. They knew Brevin's and my relationship very well, but loved to pretend like he was some saint that I'd lucked up on snagging. Also, I knew by me saying I was with Teflon, that would give him an alibi on the night of Brevin's murder; if he needed one.

"I wasn't out, *Opal,* I told you I was asleep." I shoved another piece of bread into my mouth after spreading butter on it.

"You cheated on my brother. I knew you weren't about shit."

Shrugging while holding the bread I said, "I'm not shit? You left to another state and no one even knew if you were still alive honey. And frankly… no one gave a fuck either." I whispered the last part.

"My baby was good to you!" Mrs. Williamson interjected, eyes watering up.

"Ohh yeah he was, especially when he broke my wrist, caused internal bruising, blacked my eye, oh and I knew it was really love when he killed our child that I still had to deliver," I smiled, speaking sarcastically. "And yet, you did nothing but pat him on the back for all of it."

"You disrespected him so you got what you deserved! My son was a good man who got pushed to edge constantly by some slut!"

"Excuse me!" I called out to our waitress as she walked to another table. "Can you make mine to go please, and give me a separate check?"

"Absolutely," the waitress nodded and continued to the other table before going to the back.

"A good man cheats and beats on his woman huh?" I raised a brow, glancing back and forth between Breeze and Opal. Fuck calling that bitch Mrs. Williamson; the gloves were off.

"Men do that all the time! Grow up!" Breeze frowned.

"Yeah I did grow up, when I left his no good ass. And you know what, I won't be at the funeral because honestly I've wanted the mutherfucka dead for years now. So I will probably have drinks and a little get together to celebrate instead. This is really good bread by the way."

"Leave, Tatiana."

"No I want my food first and then I will leave happily."

The three of us sat in silence as they glared at me. I on the other hand would give them closed mouth smiles here and there, while continuing to tear into that good ass bread.

"Here we are, and yours to go." The waitress finally returned and placed everyone's food. Down. She pressed the check to mine on top of my plastic bag. After I looked at it, I peeled off one hundred dollars and told her to keep the change.

"Oh and by the way, I'm pregnant." I said, before grabbing my food and switching out while texting Cecily for a ride.

I bet I won't be wasting any more of my time on funeral activities.

CHAPTER TWENTY ONE

Cecily Salecito

$\mathcal{I}$ stood under the showerhead wondering why Ryan never made it home. He'd never *not* come home. No matter how late, he always made it. I shook my head at my thoughts, trying to keep myself from thinking the worst and crying. Maybe the fact that Brevin was gone had changed things a bit for him, and he needed to work more. I was hoping that was the case because if Ryan had another bitch, I would be so heartbroken it wouldn't make any sense.

"What are you thinking about?" Ryan's deep voice jolted me from my thoughts as he wrapped his hands around my body, just as I'd started to lather up.

"Where were you?" I inquired, scared to look at him for some reason as he nibbled on my ear and let his big hand travel down my stomach until it was in between my legs.

"Slept in the living room. I passed out waiting on a phone call."

I didn't know if he was lying because with the way our apartment was set up, you couldn't see into the living room if you went straight to the bathroom like I'd done.

Before I could say anything, he bent me over and slid inside of me from behind. I gripped the handle connected to the shower doors, as he held tightly onto my waist and pumped me vigorously. I hadn't slept with him in a couple days, and it was obvious I'd been craving him by how quickly I came. My body jumped and shivered as I released my nectar onto his thick pole, while he groped my ass roughly.

Ryan knew just how to touch me in ways that would have me ready to say and do whatever the fuck he wanted me to, no matter how crazy.

"Mmm, shit," I cried as he slammed into me, slapping our skin together loudly.

"Damn," he moaned lowly, gripping my hips tighter as he fucked me harder.

My jaw stayed open as orgasm after orgasm, spilled from my body. My legs were so fucking weak, that if he wasn't grasping my hips so tightly, they'd buckle under me.

"Oh fuck, mmm," I whimpered, body stiffening up as Ryan went to town, sending chills throughout my body.

He held my shoulder as he thrust into me, just before he filled me up with his seeds. I stayed in the same position, breathing heavily as he slowly pulled out of me. I could feel my juices dripping down my legs because of how hard and how frequently I'd cum.

As I allowed myself to gain some composure, Ryan washed himself off and then I did the same before we got out.

"I can take Rye to school, and then you can pick him up," he said, checking his handsome self out in the mirror.

Ryan was fine as hell with his smooth brown skin, low cut fade, deep dimples, and the most perfect teeth you'd ever see. He was a little over six feet, and his body was nicely built but not too much.

When we first got together I didn't know how or why he was interested in me, but he eventually broke me up from that. Don't get me wrong, I'm beautiful, but I didn't have much going for me when Ryan and I met. From day one he was about his money and always had it, so I didn't know why a fine ass nigga wanted a girl like me who was still living with her mother, didn't have a car or a job, and was what weak niggas liked to call fat when they couldn't fuck me. But he did and now we had a beautiful son.

"Okay that's fine. I will pick him up." I tightened my towel around my body. "What would you like for dinner tonight?" I hugged his body from behind as he finished brushing his teeth.

"I have to— nachos. You think you can make nachos?"

I knew he was about to blow me off, but I was too happy that he'd change his mind to bring it up. He was trying so I was gonna try not to bite his head off.

"Seriously Ryan? That's all you and Rye wanna eat is Mexican food. You know I'm half Puerto Rican right?" I joked, watching him swish around the mouthwash.

"Yeah I fucking know." He moved around me after kissing my forehead.

I brushed, flossed, and rinsed, then went into the bedroom to get dressed. He was done before me, so he kissed my lips gently and then went to get Rye up and bathe him. He was a well-behaved boy, so Ryan didn't have to worry about him messing up his clothes or anything. Once Rye was bathed and had brushed his teeth and dressed, they both left, with Ryan and Rye both yelling bye from the front of the apartment.

I had on everything but my shoes, so I decided to go make myself some tea before work. As I passed the living room, I noticed the couch was the same as I'd left it last night. Maybe I was being paranoid again, but not a thing had moved since yesterday. I would think that if he'd slept there, at least a pillow or something would be in a different spot, but no. Even my watch that I'd taken off while watching TV in the living room was still in the same place. It was too shiny to miss, so if he'd laid down he would have moved it first.

Relax Cecily, I told myself.

I made myself some tea, downed it, and then went to put my shoes on before going to my nail shop for work.

***

That afternoon...

I was walking inside of Tremont Montessori to pick Rye up from preschool, when I saw someone that looked familiar. I realized it was my ex boyfriend Micah, so I tried to just keep walking and not say anything.

"Cecily?" I heard him call my name, just as I passed him. Closing my eyes tightly, I paused for a few and then turned to face him.

"Micah, hey!"

"Damn, I mean wow you look nice." He grinned. He reminded me of a younger version of Terrence Howard, light eyes and everything.

"Thanks so do you. Is this your daughter?" I looked down at the little girl holding his hand.

"No, no this is my niece; my brother Malachi's daughter. He had another engagement so I had to pick her up. Say hi, Malika."

"Hi," the little girl waved her hand shyly.

"So I'm guessing you have a kid?" He asked.

"Yeah I have a son; Rye."

"Well I will let you get to him then. Maybe we can have lunch or something."

"I would love to, but I have a boyfriend and I don't think he'd be okay with it. Not to say that you're interested or anything, he just wouldn't like it."

"I understand. I probably wouldn't want you to go if you were mine either."

Micah and I used to think we were gonna get married, but I left him when I met Ryan. Micah was too much of a good guy, and I preferred Ryan's thug demeanor. Not to mention I was thrilled that someone of Ryan's caliber wanted me. I ended up cheating on Micah, and then eventually Ryan made me choose and it was obvious who I went with.

"Yeah…" We looked at one another for a little longer. "Well it was nice seeing you, Micah."

"Likewise."

I watched him for a moment, and then went to get my son. Right now was not the time for me to be running into old flames; not when my man wasn't handling his business on the home front.

CHAPTER TWENTY TWO

Teflon

"Tef," Tatiana moaned softly as she massaged my hair.

I had my head between her hips, feasting on my favorite. The further I buried my face, the wider her legs opened, and the more labored her breathing became. Her small soft hands caressed my head as I collapsed my lips around her clit to suck softly. Her small soft thighs fit perfectly into my hands as I groped and massaged them roughly while attacking her pussy.

"Oh my gosh," she let out a moan that came from deep within as I ate her pussy like it would be the last time.

She came hard as hell, clamping her thighs against the sides of my head, and gripping my hair in her hands as she clenched her teeth while looking down at me. Her body jerked slightly, as I licked her clean, enjoying the taste of her.

I pulled my head from between her legs and turned her body to the side so I could kiss up her sexy ass thighs. As I was just getting into the shit, someone started beating on my front door.

"Fuck," I mumbled, getting out the bed, slipping some boxers on and grabbing my gun.

Tatiana covered her naked body with the comforter, as I made my way to the front of my apartment. Taking my safety off of the gun, I looked through the peephole and my jaw dropped when I saw it was my trouble making ass brother Torrey. I forgot he got out today. Actually I remembered but I was hoping if I didn't mention it, I wouldn't see his ass. I should have known better though.

"Open this door baby bro!" he barked.

"Shit," I shouted under my breath, before unlocking the door.

"What's good?" He grinned, just as I heard the shower come on. I guess Tatiana decided to start that shit without me.

"How you get here, Torrey? You bet not have told one of yo' weak ass homies where I stay at man."

"Nah I didn't. Cameron dropped me off."

"Ma must have told her where I live."

"Yeah she did." He looked past me. "So can I come in or what nigga? I'm starving."

I moved back so he could come in, and he surveyed my spot until he made it to the kitchen. He immediately opened the fridge and started to pull shit out, so I went to the bathroom to brush my teeth and then join Tatiana in the shower.

"Who was it?" She asked, as she rinsed the soap off her little sexy body. She was starting to show a little bit, and that shit had me excited like a muthafucka.

"Torrey."

"Crazy shit starting Torrey?"

"Yes." I dropped my head and she reached up to caress my cheek before kissing my lips.

"Don't worry. Maybe he's changed now that he's out, Tre'Wayne."

"No he hasn't. My brother will forever be a nigga who causes havoc wherever the fuck he goes, trust me."

"Have some faith."

We finished our shower then got dressed, and by that time my brother was on my couch holding three damn sandwiches, and a big ass glass of pop.

"Damn nigga, that's how you eat in other muthafuckas houses?" I frowned, holding Tatiana's hand.

He paused upon seeing her, and set his plate to the side.

"And that's how you speak in front of a beautiful ass lady?" He rose to his feet and made his way over to us. "Torrey." He reached for her free hand.

"Nice to meet you, Torrey. I'm Tatiana, Tre'Wayne's girlfriend."

"Aight so that's enough of that. Wrap them fucking sandwiches up and come on so I can take yo' ass home," I said, making Tatiana chuckle and head towards the kitchen.

"How you know I ain't been home yet?" Torrey inquired with a frown.

"Because I know you, now come the fuck on."

I started out the door as Torrey followed me, taking my plate and glass like a fucking hooligan.

His girl Audrina had been waiting on that nigga since he got sentenced and he had the audacity to keep her and my niece waiting on him. Torrey was the worst nigga and I doubt he would ever change.

"So what's the deal with some work?" He asked as soon as I pulled out onto the street, headed to Audrina's spot.

"Fuck you asking me for?"

"Because I know you got something for me. You always got some shit, Tef. So whatever got you that nice spot and that pretty little bitch back home—"

"Who the fuck you calling a bitch, Torrey?" I glanced over at him as we sat at the red light. I moved his hand when he tried to turn my radio up.

"My bad, I'm sorry." He sighed and chuckled, while shaking his head. "Damn you know I ain't calling her a bitch like that. She's pretty as hell, but I need a little more to grab on than what she got."

"I'm happy you feel that way. I don't need you looking at her because I might have to hurt you. She's perfect to me though."

"Must be why you knocked her up and acting like a little bitch over her. I ain't never heard you talk like this about Kayla."

"Shut yo' ass up and who told you about the baby?"

"She did, pulling out all that damn food just for some breakfast for her little ass."

We stopped and got him something to eat, and as soon as I pulled up in front of Audrina's house, I hit the locks so he could get his ass out. I had shit to handle today and didn't need his ass on my fucking hip like a baby.

"Damn, I get the hint. But aye, when are you gon' talk to me about some work? You know with my record I can't get no regular job."

"Torrey man I don't know. I'm kind of hot right now. Maybe once I get everything settled and in order I'll have some shit for you. But you need to make sure you're ready to work. You fuck up once and I'm letting yo' ass go. I swear to God."

"I told you I ain't on that tip no more man. I'm ready to turn my life around as much as I can."

"Well show me by treating your family like they matter. The first person you should have seen when you got out was Audrina and Tori nigga."

"Yeah yeah. Hit me up though. Oh shit I need a phone. Think you can handle that for me?"

"Yeah I'll be back around by here later with something for you. Get out my car man."

"Aight."

As soon as he got close enough to his door, I sped off, headed to a meeting with Merce, Groove, Garrett, and Mack. As I came to a stop sign, my phone started to ring, so I answered it without looking, using my Bluetooth.

"Hello?"

"Hey boo!" Kayla shrieked.

"Kayla, what's up man? I'm driving."

"I want to see you."

"Well I don't plan on going to California anytime soon."

"Don't have to, I'm here in Ohio."

"What? When? And for how long?"

"As long as I want. So when can I see you? I'm free tonight of course."

"I'll let you know, Kayla. I gotta go. I'll hit you later."

"Tef—"

I hung up quickly as fuck.

Shit…

CHAPTER TWENTY THREE

Torrey German

I watched Tre'Wayne's old annoying ass speed down the street, as I waited for Audrina to open the door. That nigga always acted like he was the older brother, ever since we were kids. I wasn't fucking with that shit though, never had. I was the oldest so I ran shit.

I'd heard from inside the jail cell that Teflon was making moves with that Brevin cat, and if he didn't put me on, I'd find my way in somehow. Clearly he didn't know what the fuck he was doing because he'd gotten our little brother killed; him and his little bitch according to my mama.

"Torrey," Audrina whispered, eyes wide and glazed over. She unlocked the screen and stepped out to hug my neck.

"How you doing?"

"Good now."

I pressed my lips against hers and picked her up to carry her inside. I locked the door with my free hand, and then joined it with the other to caress her body. We fell onto the couch, and I began to run my hands up her dress, but she stopped me. I didn't know why but I'm sure it was because of some bullshit.

"Torrey, don't you wanna see Tori?" She quizzed.

"I will, after we do this."

"You haven't seen her since she was a newborn. She's five years old now and barely knows you since you took us off the visiting list."

"Damn! Why do you have to run yo' fucking mouth so much!"

"Run my mouth? I'm asking you to see your daughter because you haven't!"

WHAM!

I went across Audrina's face with the quickness because clearly her muthafucking ass had forgotten who she was talking to.

WHAM!

My head flew back when Audrina punched my ass, catching me off guard like a muthafucka. I could feel the warm blood dripping from my nose onto my lips as I stared at her like she'd lost her got damn mind.

Audrina rose to her feet, not even fazed by the split lip I'd just given her. "Yeah things have changed nigga. Won't be no more of that shit. If you're gonna stay here with me you better grow the fuck up and keep your hands to your damn self, and contribute financially. If you can't do either, not only will I hit your ass back, but you won't be getting any pussy, and you'll be living on the fucking curb."

"Aye who the fuck you talking to!" I shot up off the couch and towered over her. She didn't cower one bit under me and the shit was pissing me off!

"You're the only nigga in here right? I've stuck by you this whole time even through the infidelity, the domestic abuse, you being broker than a two dollar hoe, and even your jail stint which was a result of you doing dumb shit on the daily that didn't bring you any money."

My skin began to heat up as her words seeped into my fucking mind like poison. I wasn't feeling this new bitch she'd become, and I wasn't about to let her ass come at me like that.

"Mommy," a little voice bounced off the walls before I could respond to Audrina's disrespectful ass.

When I looked behind her, I saw Tori, my little girl looking just like me with the same deep chocolate complexion, and big pretty brown eyes. She had a little curly ponytail on top of her head, and was wearing a pink dress with matching sandals.

Audrina dabbed her lip and then turned around to greet Tori.

"Hey baby, come here." She squatted down and waited for Tori to come closer. When she did, Audrina picked her up and said, "Tori, baby this is your daddy."

My daughter just stared at me, and when I reached to touch her she moved away. That shit immediately got me hot, but I was gonna try and keep my cool because I didn't feel like boxing with Audrina's ass again.

"You have other niggas around her?" I hissed, all kinds of shit circling my mind.

"No, Torrey. She doesn't know you! You got locked up when she was three weeks old."

"So! You brought her to see me in the pen, and I'm sure you showed her some fucking pictures!"

"Okay, maybe you need to leave and cool down, because you can't be here with all this hostility."

"Yeah maybe so." I snatched my jacket off the couch. "Don't wait up."

"I won't. Remember you don't have a key Torrey, so don't stay out too late. And definitely don't come back here smelling like another bitch or you'll be camping out on the porch."

I gripped the doorknob and closed my eyes, taking a deep breath before I left.

I didn't have a car and no way of getting one, especially without a damn phone, so I just started to walk. When I made it to One Stop Liquor around the corner on Buckeye Road, I went inside and pocketed a beer before slipping out. Didn't have no fucking cash so what did you expect?

"Shit," I mumbled as I leaned up against the outside of the store, and cracked open the beer.

I wish the fuck the owner would come out here and say some shit to me. I was irritated already from Teflon and Audrina, so the next muthafucka to come at me foul was bound to get beat to death.

As I downed my beer and nodded my head up to a couple people that walked by, a big black truck pulled up on me. I admit I tensed up a little bit, because I didn't know what the fuck or who the fuck they were here for. My mind raced trying to remember if I'd left any enemies before I went to jail, but the only ones I did leave weren't riding clean like this.

The back window finally rolled down and some big meatball muthafucka with more gold around his neck than pawnshop, smiled.

"You Torrey German?" He quizzed in his Latin accent.

"Who the fuck wants to know?"

"Me. I have a proposition for you. That's if you want to make some money, and a lot of it."

"Tef sent you?"

"We can talk more if you get in the car."

I looked to my right and then my left, before lifting off the wall and making my way towards the car. I hopped inside and said, "Aight talk." Before taking a sip of beer.

"I do know Teflon, but from back in California."

I snapped my neck to look at him. "Shit you're Luis? The nigga that had his pockets fat on the West?"

"No Luis was my brother, but he's passed on and now and what was his is mine. We have a lot in common Torrey."

"We do?"

"Yes, we're both always living in the shadows of our brothers, even though they're extremely inadequate." He stared straight ahead as he sighed. "I'm no longer living in Luis' shadow though, and you dont have to continue to live in Teflon's."

"Why you wanna help me?"

"Because I see the potential in you, and your brother double crossed me."

"You don't even know me."

"I know everyone that I want to get to know. How do you think I found you here? How do you think I knew when you were getting out?"

Taking another sip of beer I asked, "Well what you got in mind?"

He grinned widely as hell so I returned the gesture. If Teflon didn't want to help me get this money, then I'd do the shit on my fucking own; even if it meant going against him.

CHAPTER TWENTY FOUR

Merce

"It's gonna happen tonight and I'm too ready," Teflon spoke into the phone, as I laid on Jadynn's lap, allowing her to rub my head. I don't know what it was about that shit but I loved when she did it.

"Nigga beyond. I'm so tired of talking and thinking about this nigga it's ridiculous," I sucked my teeth, and winked playfully at Jadynn who chuckled.

"Well be ready. After tonight I need to celebrate, and then it's right back to work. Somebody is feeding the streets again and we need to find out who."

"Yeah well you know who is gonna get us connected."

"Oh I know."

"Aight then my nigga, see you tonight."

I hung up with Teflon and closed my eyes at the feeling of Jadynn's soft ass hands. Taking her free one, I brought it my lips and kissed the back of it. As I did so, I my phone started to ring and I saw it was

Savannah's ass so I quickly turned it over and hit the lock button to silence it.

"Who was that?" She asked.

"Little brother." I was honestly surprised Savannah hadn't tried Jadynn yet, and it was good for her ass not to.

"Where is he? I would expect him to be back there in the extra room playing his loud ass music."

Chuckling I said, "I know. I told his ass to enroll in school and get a job, so I guess he did that. He ain't asked me for no bread in a minute."

"Well that's good. See I told you he may get it together."

"What about yo' sibling situation? You still not fucking with yo' sister?"

"Nope."

"It ain't because you care about that nigga right?" I raised a brow, intertwining our hands and keeping intense eye contact with her pretty ass.

"Not at all. But she betrayed me and I'm not ready to talk to her. I don't know if I'll ever be ready to talk to her."

"Understandable."

She leaned down to touch my face before her lips pressed against mine. As we got into the shit, making my dick hard as a missile, I heard something hitting my front door. It was subtle as fuck though, so I paused for a minute to make sure.

"What?" Jadynn inquired.

"You hear that? It's like—"

"Sebastian!!!!!" I heard some hood rat yell from outside the door.

"Shit," I mumbled, hopping off the couch and darting to the door. Looking out the peephole, I saw some bitch with a box of something, throwing shit out of it at my door. "Aye what the fuck is wrong with you?" I snatched the door open and glared down at her stupid ass, seeing that she was holding a box of tacks.

Really? Tacks?

"Wh-where is Sebastian?" She panted, looking like she had just shit herself.

"He ain't here! When you go to people's houses you need knock like you got some muthafucking sense! Next time it won't be me talking it, it'll be my .45!"

"Just tell him, Phoenix came by."

"I ain't telling him shit."

"Why ca—"

I slammed the door in her face, and as I made my way further back into the apartment I saw Jadynn chuckling and shaking her head at me.

"You're so damn mean."

"I don't give a fuck. Bitch need to act like she got some sense and she'll get to speak to a muthcafucka with sense."

She just chuckled as I grabbed my phone back up and dialed Sebastian's ass. Of course he didn't answer, even after the fifth call. I gave up because I couldn't deal with his ass right now.

Quickly grabbing my hoodie and my keys, I walked back out to the front to get Jadynn so we could go get something to eat.

"Is that your brother right there?" Jadynn pointed down an alleyway as I drove by, on the way to the restaurant.

I looked closer, slowing down, and I realized it was definitely his ass. I cut a few cars off making a U-turn, and hopped out leaving the engine running.

"Sebastian!"

He looked at me and then took off running but didn't get far. I snatched his ass up by the collar as he hollered and called me all types of names that were about to have me going upside his fucking head.

"Aye man, come on!"

"Get in the fucking car!" I roared.

"I ain't getting in shit!" As soon as the words left his mouth I had my piece to his head, in broad fucking daylight. "I can't stand yo' ass!" He sucked his teeth and hopped into the car.

I drove back to my spot, and as soon as we got up inside I started patting his pockets. When I felt what he was holding, I snatched that shit up out.

"Who the fuck you working for dummy?"

"Nobody! I work for myself!" He barked.

"Oh so you grew this shit on a farm? Answer the fucking question before I box yo' dumb ass head nigga!"

"I don't know man! I got the shit from Bobby, and all I do is sell, give him the cut, and he takes it to whomever the fuck he works for I swear! Why you tripping? You told me to make some money and now

I'm doing it!"

"Not illegally! I told you that! Get the fuck out my face before I sock yo' ass."

"I'm leaving—"

"If you leave don't come back, Bash. You gon' move the fuck in with our parents. I'm not dealing with this shit no more. If you wanna sell drugs and get stuck in some shit like me, then by all means, but you ain't gon' do the shit under my damn roof."

"Fine with me." Was all he said as he stormed back out.

"You're gonna let him go?" Jadynn pointed.

"He's a grown ass man baby, and I'm tired. I'd like to save some energy for when you have *my* kids." I walked over and hugged her from behind.

"Wait what?" She chuckled.

"You heard me." I started to kiss on her neck.

Teflon mentioned that some muthafucka was feeding the streets and clearly it was true because my brother was working for him. I just needed to figure out who the fuck it was that thought they were about to step into Brevin's shoes, because they a rude awakening coming.

CHAPTER TWENTY SIX

Groove

Teflon, Merce, and I pulled up to Brevin's old warehouse where Mack and Garrett had Brevin's *living* team waiting on us. We'd gotten rid of a lot of them when robbing and destroying traps, but because Teflon flew off the muthafucking handle and murked Brevin too early, there were still some people loyal to him. So now we needed Mack to help us convert them, otherwise we'd have to murk their asses too somehow. I wasn't really with the latter plan because we needed people to feed the blocks and shit, and recruiting wasn't in the time budget as of right now. Not to mention, we needed to spend time figuring out who the hell was trying to be our competition.

"Y'all each got two weapons right? Just in case this shit goes completely left?" Teflon asked, looking in the rearview mirror. Merce replied to him, and I nodded since he was looking at me.

We got out of the car, and went around to the side like Mack had advised. The plan was for Mack to convince these niggas, and once we were sure we had them in our pocket, we'd get rid of Mack's ass. He couldn't be trusted if he would switch up on Brevin so easily. We needed niggas on our team that would have our back even if we were six feet deep in the grave.

Merce swore that tonight would go as planned because a nigga like Mack was too damn scared and bitch made to hold the reigns on anything. I just hoped he was right because a shoot out wasn't in my plans tonight. I had enough shit going on and getting shot wasn't one of them. It wasn't even the fact of me getting shot either, it was more of that I didn't want both Anya and Cecily trying to roll up and visit my ass.

We entered the big ass warehouse, and walked through the door to the left to see Mack and Garrett in a room of about 10 niggas.

"Everybody, as y'all know this is Teflon and Merce. Y'all pretty much know Groove," Mack gestured towards us as we walked further into the room. Garrett was mean mugging us with his gay ass, but it didn't matter because he'd be dead soon too.

"What's up?" They all said somewhat simultaneously.

"Sup," Teflon nodded, and Merce and I followed suit, keeping our distance because neither party was sure yet.

"I was just explaining to the fellas here that y'all would be taking over for Brevin since his passing. They were a little apprehensive, but I assured them that shit would be good, even better."

"Y'all got any questions? Concerns?" Teflon spoke up, eyeing the room.

"Yeah I hope you ain't planning on falling back like Brevin did once the money starts flowing again, because that shit caused me to fall behind on a lot of shit and I ain't appreciate that," one dude said. Super light skinned nigga with light eyes and tattoos all over his face. He bore a permanent scowl, and I could tell by the way that he was eyeing us that he didn't trust too many muthafuckas.

"Nah I definitely won't be letting that happen. Shit is gon' be different as fuck, and it won't be just one person making all the damn decisions; stupid ones at that," Teflon replied.

"Didn't you and Brevin have some kind of beef? How the fuck we know you ain't kill him?" Some dark skinned dude with dreads inquired.

"If I did would you care?" Teflon folded his arms. The dude with dreads just chuckled and sat back in his chair. "Look I know this shit seems weird, but if y'all are anything like I think y'all are, all you give a fuck about is the money. Brevin hadn't been doing shit for the past couple of months but spending money, drinking, and fucking bitches. Not only will shit be back to normal, but it'll be better."

"You got a connect?" Some Hispanic dude inquired.

"Let us worry about that. We just need to make sure y'all are ready," Merce replied.

I didn't feel the need to say too much because I was more of the manager of shit, like I was with Brevin. I made sure he stayed on his toes, or tried to, and handled shit that didn't necessarily have shit to do with the drugs. I was gonna do the same for my cousin and Merce, making sure them niggas kept their heads in the game and hopefully didn't backslide like Brevin's bitch ass.

The dudes as well as Garrett, left after two hours straight of Teflon going over how shit was supposed to work now that he was taking over.

We made sure that Brevin didn't have anybody out there looking for my cousin since it was rumored they had beef. But since it was only a 'rumor', the dude with dreads explained that we'd been looking over our shoulder for nothing. He and the Hispanic guy also agreed to take Carnie, Brevins' street spy, out, as soon as he showed his face.

Honestly this meeting went way smoother than what I'd expected, and I was thankful for that shit. I was also happy that we didn't have to low-key look over our shoulders anymore, fearing that niggas would come back to enact revenge on Brevin's behalf. I knew his little niggas, but I wasn't in tune with them like Mack so it wasn't like I could walk up and get the info I needed, or rally them up like he did.

"Why was it only 10 muthafuckas here?" I asked Mack.

"They each have a team of their own. We tell them something and they pass it down. We don't need every muthafucka we have working for us in here tonight."

"You know anything about the nigga who's pushing shit now?" Merce inquired.

"Nope. I know he's new though."

We chopped it up for a little longer, and then went out to our cars.

Once we got inside, Teflon said, "Man had I known that this nigga didn't have anybody fucking with him like that, I would have been killed his ass. I'm mad I let that nigga live so fucking long."

"What we gon' do about Garrett?" Merce asked as Teflon drove.

"Shit where the hell has his ass been?" I frowned.

"No idea. I ain't seen or heard from that nigga since Brevin,

Teflon, and I popped up over there." Merce shook his head.

Teflon drove me to Anya's since he and Merce lived in the same building, and when he came to a stop I said, "Aye if Cecily calls Jadynn or Tatiana, tell them to tell her I had to take care of something for y'all tonight."

I loved Cecily a lot, and was realizing I loved Anya too. Only reason I was staying with Anya most nights was because I could easily convince Cecily that I was working. Anya wasn't going for that shit because like a dumb ass, I would confide in her about my work life when Cecily was stressing me out.

"Nigga what are you doing with this girl? I thought Anya was just a little something on the side. You coming home to her now?" Teflon frowned, looking at me through the rearview. He knew nothing about my daughter Brin.

"Shit is complicated. Just do what I said for me aight?" I hopped out the car not caring to wait for a response, and then used my key to enter Anya's crib.

I locked the door behind me, turned my phone on Do Not Disturb, and then went into Brin's room to check on her. She was sleeping peacefully as fuck, making me yawn, so after kissing her soft cheeks, I went to the bathroom to take a quick shower. When I got out, I grabbed some boxers that I bought to keep over here, slipped them on, and then climbed into the bed.

Hugging Anya from behind, I kissed her shoulder, and she got comfortable in my arms. I hated to say it, but nothing felt wrong about this shit…

CHAPTER TWENTY SEVEN

Jadynn

The next evening…

I plopped down on my couch, and immediately removed my shoes. Frowning down at my feet as I moved them back and forth, I couldn't help but wish Merce was here to massage them. I'd literally been running around all fucking day, unexpectedly. Had I known I would need to run so many errands for work, I would have definitely chosen to wear some flats, or even a nice pair of sneakers. From now on, back up shoes and outfits would be already in my car.

I got up and went to my bedroom because I wanted to take some candles to the bathroom. I was gonna have a nice hot bath in some Epsom salt, before Merce came over tonight. I just needed him to fuck me, and fuck me well which he never had a problem doing.

I never understood girls who would say they couldn't leave a man because the dick was too bomb… until now. The way that man made me cum, it would break my heart to leave that shit behind. Not to mention, I loved his personality, and I think I was falling in love too. This shit was a dangerous ass game I tell you.

KNOCK! KNOCK!

I set the candles down in my bathroom and started towards the door. Before looking through the peephole, I checked the time on the cable box to make sure I wasn't tripping. It was only 6:30pm, and Merce wasn't supposed to be here until 8pm. When I looked out, I didn't see anyone, so I grabbed my extra pepper spray sitting on the end table, and opened the door.

"Ahh!" I jumped back when I saw a big ass black bird with a knife plunged in its chest. "What the fuck?!" I panted, hand over my chest.

"You okay?" My neighbor Artie asked. He was an old white man who dressed like he ran a farm, but ironically smelled good as hell all the time.

"Uhh…" I simply pointed downward. "Did you see someone come by here just now?" I asked as he bent down to pick it up with his BARE hands.

"Nope. I just walked out when I heard you scream. You know it's my duty to protect the pretty girls in this building," he laughed, showing all of the teeth he had *left*.

"Well thanks, Artie."

"Anytime. You have a goodnight now."

I watched him walk off with the bird, and then take the knife out its chest. He wiped the blood off on his overalls, and then put the knife into his pocket. Shaking my head, I closed the door, and even put the chain on. I was still shaken up a bit, but I figured some stupid ass weird kids were just playing a dumb joke on me.

I went back to gather my bubble bath and everything else I needed, and just as I got undressed, someone knocked on my door again. Snatching my cloth robe off the back of the bathroom door, I stormed to the door, grabbed my spray, quickly yanked the chain off, and opened it. When I saw my sister there, rubbing her small belly, my breath got caught in my throat.

"I hope you'll give me a chance to talk before you spray me with that."

"What, Paige?"

"Can I?"

I stood there pondering for a few moments, and then backed up so she could come in. I don't know why I was allowing her in, but I figured if I let that asswipe Russell talk to me, I could let her hoe ass do the same.

"Hurry up because I'm only giving you five minutes." I closed the door, locking it.

"Jadynn, I know what I did to you was wrong, but there has to be a way for me to fix this. I don't want to have you out of my life, and I want my child to know you as well."

"Paige, as long as you go to bed at night with a man who raped me, you and I can never be close. Plus, I will never be able to trust you again."

"Jadynn, he's sorry, he really is! He told me that he came to you and apologized! Yes, what he did was wrong, but we all do things that we regret and want second chances for!"

"Not rape! I did not rape anyone, I did not kill anyone, and I have never done anything that damn near ruined somebody! Do not come into my house telling me to forgive someone who violated me, just because you're too weak to leave his stupid ass alone! And for your information, Paige, the only reason his ass apologized was because he wanted to get back together!"

"I don't believe that, Jadynn."

"Of course you don't. You only believe what he tells you. Paige, please leave."

"Why are you so jealous of me?"

Laughing because I was so appalled, I couldn't help but to let my eyes run amuck all over her face, hoping to find that she was just being funny.

"Something is really wrong with you, Paige. And like I just said, I'd like you to leave and please don't ever come back over here again. If you do I might whoop your ass, and I know you don't want that. You didn't take it too well the last time."

"When my daughter grows up and doesn't know who you are, you're gonna regret it."

"And you can just tell her why. If not, when she grows up to be a woman, I will happily let her know that her slut of a mother chose her rapist boyfriend over me."

Paige just shook her head and got up from the couch. I saw she was having a hard time because of her belly, but I didn't give a fuck. As soon as she made it across the threshold, I slammed the door and locked it, then took my ass to the bathroom for a bath. My bath wasn't even as relaxing because all I kept thinking about was that conversation between Paige and I.

By the time I'd gotten out, dried off, and spread lotion on my body, I came out the bathroom to see Merce lying in my bed texting on his phone.

"When did you get here?"

"Like five minutes ago. Come here." He set his phone on the table next to the bed.

I tightened my towel as I rounded the bed, and as soon as I got closer, he yanked me on top of him. Keeping eye contact with me, he released himself, and then picked me up a little before bringing me down on him. I bit down hard on my lip as he filled me up, eyes never leaving mine as he guided my hips. I wasn't quite juiced yet, but damn was I getting there. And just sitting on it had me ready to explode already.

"Mmm," I finally let out, pressing my palm into his chest as I began to take control of my movements.

He grasped my hips and pressed himself upward, going into me even further than he already was. My body trembled when I released, prompting him to moan lowly as he finally removed my towel. I rocked my hips faster, going up and down, liking the way his face twisted up and the way his deep moans flowed through his sexy lips. A tingling sensation began to race through my body as I felt myself reaching my peak.

"Fuck, I'm about to nut," Merce grumbled, pressing his head back into the pillow as his big hands gripped me even tighter.

I picked up the pace, feeling my orgasm on the horizon as well, and before I knew it we were both crying out in pleasure. I fell to the side of him, and we both laid there panting heavily. We finally got up once we'd gained some composure, and while he showered, I cleaned myself up and brushed my teeth.

"Why you so quiet?" he asked as we laid in my bed with the lights out, trying to go to sleep.

"I'm thinking about pressing charges against Russell."

"I thought you didn't want to."

"I didn't but now I do. For some reason, him getting beat up just wasn't enough for me. Even though I was initially upset when you did it. What do you think?"

"It's a good idea. You should have done the shit a long time ago, but I understood why you held back." He kissed the top of my head.

"Yeah well not anymore."

It was time I cut Paige completely the fuck off, and make Russell pay even more than he did. It wasn't fair for them to just run through the daisies together after what they'd done to me.

CHAPTER TWENTY EIGHT

Tatiana

I sat at my desk, reading over some emails sent to me by the food critic, the bloggers, and a few photographers that were gonna be at Zeus' opening. As I looked through my calendar to make sure I had the dates right, someone knocked on my office door. I yelled come in without, looking, and as I hit send on the hundredth damn email I'd sent today, I turned in my chair to see who it was.

"Eddie, who are these people?" I frowned, seeing Eddie's short ass with two big black guys in suits standing behind him. They reminded me of the Men In Black, even though their suits were an ashy beige color.

"Tatiana, these are detectives, and they're here to talk to you. Is now a good time?"

"My lunch is in 30 minutes, so if we can finish up before that then yes, that's perfectly fine." I nodded, trying to hide the fact that I was slightly nervous.

"Great. Excuse me." Eddie slipped out, closing my office door behind him.

"Have a seat gentlemen." I gestured towards the chairs that were positioned in front of my desk.

"Thanks, Miss Drew." The black guy with a thick mustache spoke up first. He reminded me a lot of my father. "We just wanted to ask you some questions about, Brevin Williamson, your fiancé."

"I know who he is."

"I would hope so," he chuckled but I kept a straight face. "Where were you the night he was murdered?"

"Well, like I told my ex soon-to-be mother in law, you know the one who sent you, I was with my new boyfriend at his apartment."

"New boyfriend?"

"Yes, is that a problem?"

"Well, I uhh… I guess I just assumed that you and Mr. Williamson were exclusive. It just comes as a surprise that's all."

"Were you this surprised when you found him dead in a bed with another woman? Or was that considered okay since he's a man?" I smiled, waiting for their response.

"I wasn't actually, but that was because when I arrived to the scene I didn't know his relationship status. But Miss Drew, did your boyfriend ever leave the apartment at any time?"

"Nope."

"Did Brevin have any enemies?" the other one finally spoke up.

"Oh plenty, especially the boyfriends of the women he'd slept with during our relationship." I picked my glass of water up and took a sip.

"Okay… uh, can we get your boyfriend's contact information just so we can verify your alibi?"

"Of course." I set the glass of water down, and began to write Teflon's cellphone number on a Post-It. I handed it over with a smile, and watched the detective look it over.

"Thank you for your time, Miss Drew."

I simply nodded and watched them leave. I wasn't worried one bit because Teflon said I didn't need to be. He promised there was no way they'd find out who'd done it, because of the way he went about it. Even though I felt like he may have left something since the killing wasn't planned, I trusted his honesty.

I appreciated that about Teflon. He never hid things or tried to make something seem okay when it wasn't. If he even thought he would go to jail for this, he would have said so.

I made a few more phone calls, sent some emails, and once I was tired and starving, I looked down at my phone to see it was time for lunch.

I grabbed my purse and then made my way to Jadynn's office to see if she could come along with me.

"Hungry yet?" I smiled, leaning on her door.

"Ummm…" she scanned her desk and then checked her watch. "I guess I can go to lunch now," she smiled, before getting up from her desk.

We decided to go to The Greenhouse Tavern on 4th Street, which was like a restaurant district almost. The street was full of different restaurants, and a House of Blues was located right next door to the spot we were eating at. It was a perfect place to take a date at night. Brevin and I used to frequent this area a lot when we were happy.

"And here we go," the pretty blond waitress set our food down with a smile. "Anything else I can get for you?"

"Just some napkins please," Jadynn replied as I took a huge bite out of my burger.

"This is so—"

"Excuse me, which one of you is Tatiana Drew?" some freckle faced dude asked, eyes darting back and forth between Jadynn and I.

"I am. Do I know you?" I raised a brow.

"No, but I work for Zeus Rydell. This is for you." He handed me a gift bag.

"Oh no, I can't." I held my hands up and stared at what looked to be pretty expensive gift, even though I couldn't see exactly what it was.

"I'll just leave it. I can't return it; he'd be offended. Have a good day, Tatiana." After placing the bag on the table, the boy ran off and hopped onto his bike before speeding off.

"He couldn't even give the little nigga a whip to drive?" Jadynn turned her lip up, shoving a fry into her mouth. "Open it!" She pushed the bag towards me.

"Jadynn."

"Just open it. Shit it's here, and if it's expensive enough you can pawn it, or shit let me pawn it."

I chuckled, shaking my head at her as I dug into the bag. Pulling out the big square jewelry box, I lifted the top to see a diamond necklace.

"What is it?" Jadynn inquired since the bag was blocking her view of it. I slide the box across the table so she could see, and her jaw was basically sitting on the table. "You sure you didn't fuck him?"

"No!" I laughed. "He sent me four cases of roses too. I told Eddie and he asked me to just play nicely, and keep it professional."

"Well this nigga likes you. I thought it was simple flirting, but he's dropping racks on you which means he wants you."

"He has a girlfriend; a very jealous one at that. She let me know early on that she didn't play about her man."

"Clearly her man couldn't care less about what she doesn't play about because he's sending you gifts that he should only be sending her. You better get him under control before Teflon's ass catches wind of all this shit."

"I know."

"What'd you do with the flowers?"

"I allowed Tony to give them to his wife, even after I'd slid him $50 to toss it all."

"Scam artist," Jadynn giggled.

"Tell me about it."

Jadynn and I finished our lunch, and as soon as I got to privacy of my office, I dialed Zeus' ass from my personal office phone. I was gonna try and hold off until the party coming up, but I needed to set some damn boundaries *now* before he got us both killed.

"Did you like it?" he answered.

"Mr. Rydell, please stop with the gifts."

"You didn't like it? Every woman likes jewelry."

"Yes we do, but from a man that we're interested in, not someone that we're working with." I leaned back in my chair.

"So, you're not interested in me?"

"No, I'm not. I have a boyfriend actually who I'm pregnant by," I inhaled and exhaled sharply after I'd said it. I didn't want to tell anyone about my baby even though it was almost three months. I felt like speaking about it would fuck shit up like the last two times.

"Pregnant? Wow. I umm I had no idea."

"That's obvious, now if you'd please stop with the gifts and the flirting I would appreciate it. I just want to make sure your restaurant and brand gets the press needed to make a good impression on the dining scene, and that is it. I am not looking for anything else."

"I understand."

"I hope so."

CHAPTER TWENTY NINE

Cecily

The next morning...

"Mommy, can we get ice ream after school?" my son Rye questioned as I walked him to his preschool classroom.

"How about we make a deal? When I pick you up I'm gonna talk to your teacher and if she gives me a good report, then we can go for ice cream. So you know what that means?"

"What?" He cocked his little head, expression dull as an old knife, because he knew what I was about to say.

"That you must behave in class, and listen to your teacher when she tells you to do something, even if you don't want to."

"Okaaaay."

"Okay." I chuckled and kissed his cheek, before directing him into the class. I watched him for a little bit, and when the teacher and I made eye contact, I waved to her.

Walking back to my car, I couldn't help but think about how for the past two nights, Ryan didn't come home. I was tired of this shit, and wasn't sure how much longer I could deal with it.

After getting in my car, I sped to my nail salon on St. Clair Avenue, across from The Westin hotel. As I walked through, I made sure all my nail technicians were busy, and not cutting any corners. I took my business seriously and would fire a bitch with the quickness if she were trying to put speed over quality.

For as long as I could remember I wanted to do nails, and because I didn't have much growing up, I thought it would never happen. I'd do my homegirls nails on the side when I could afford the stuff, but I was nowhere near where I am today. I didn't like the fact that I had to thank Groove for that since he got me the space, but it'd be ungrateful for me not to.

Speaking of Groove, I was still fuming that he didn't come home last night, and hadn't come the night before, so when I got to my office I dialed Tatiana.

"Hey honey, I will be there to get my nails done tomorrow morning as promised," she answered happily.

"You better be," I chuckled. "Hey, I just wanted to ask you something really quickly. I know you're a busy bee these days so I won't be long."

"Sure, anything."

"Ryan has been busy as well, and I was just wondering if maybe he'd stayed over there with you guys, or maybe Jadynn said something about him staying with her."

"No, he hasn't. But Teflon told me one night that Groove had to take care of some things for him and Merce, and it would take him all night. I guess he's working on that. Why? Do you think otherwise?"

"Umm, no, no, I was just checking up you know."

"Is he still not spending time with you?"

"No, no he's gotten better. But there was one night he didn't come back and I'm sure it was the night that Teflon was referring to. But thanks Tati, see you tomorrow."

"Oka—"

I hung up quickly and closed my eyes, hand clutching my iPhone tightly. Hand over my mouth, I looked around my office, taking deep breaths so that I wouldn't let a tear fall. I wasn't even sure if I had anything to cry about. He could have been working all those nights he didn't come home, but something in my gut was telling me different.

KNOCK! KNOCK!

"Come in!" I called out.

"Hey boss, your client, Ashlee is here for her eyebrows." Ali, one of my nail technicians and assistant, peeked her head into my office.

"Okay, tell her to give me five minutes. Escort her to the room and get her a bottle of water please, Ali."

"Of course."

Once Ali left out, I went into my recent call list and scrolled down to Ryan's name before tapping it. I nibbled on my top lip as the phone rang and just as I was about to hang up, he answered.

"Hey baby," he sighed. It sounded like he was rushing somewhere and had finally come to a place or spot where he could talk.

"Hi, Ryan. What happened to you last night?"

"I would tell you but I don't feel like hearing you call me a liar, or tell me I sound like a broken record. So how about you tell me what you want me to say."

I jerked my neck back lightly because if I weren't mistaken, I would say homeboy had a little attitude when I was the one who deserved to be mad.

"Ryan, relax. I was just asking a question that I think I deserve the answer to. Your son asks about you at night and I'm sure he too is tired of the same lame ass excuse."

"I was working, same shit I'm doing right now. So what's up? What you need?"

"Nothing asshole." I hung up.

I sat there, leg bouncing wildly because I wanted to punch something. Quickly hopping up, I went out to handle my client's eyebrows, and then came back to my office to get on my laptop. I tracked Ryan's phone, and wrote down the vicinity it displayed. If only this shit would give exact addresses. Once I had the street along with the nearest cross street, I grabbed my purse and rushed out, locking my office.

"Ladies, I will be back soon." I rushed out and got into my car.

I didn't even wait to put on my seatbelt before I started driving. I was flooring it as I reached for it, and buckled myself in while in motion. About 18 minutes later I made it onto the street that he was supposedly at, and when I spotted his car a little ways down, I swooped behind a silver truck, parked by the curb. I waited for about 45 minutes, and just as I was about to leave, the front door to the house opened.

I swear I stopped breathing as I waited for someone to come out. My eyes were wide as hell, and I was positive I hadn't blinked once. Ryan finally stepped out, looking sexy as always. For some reason his attire, hoodie, jeans, and sneakers, made me feel like this was about some kind of hood business. That was until some girl with a short haircut, stepped closer into the threshold, and he leaned down to kiss her. I felt my eyebrows raise as my stomach started to twist and turn.

The way he draped his arms over her shoulders, while she hugged his torso, and the way they kissed let me know she wasn't just some side chick. He had feelings for this girl, and probably loved her. Just the thought of him dismissing me the way he had on the phone earlier, because he wanted to be with her, made me feel like shit. I'd literally just started getting comfortable in our relationship, and just stopped feeling like he was too good for me, and now this.

I thought about confronting her, but I would hold off on that until I got myself together. I refused to let that bitch see me crying and shit. When I came at her, I was gonna be poised and unbothered.

To humor myself, I pulled my phone from my purse and texted Ryan.

Me: Coming home tonight?

I watched him text on his phone as he walked to his car.

Ryan: Doubt it. I'm working. I will take Rye to school though. And sorry about earlier ma, I love you.

Shaking my head, I just chuckled and backed out of my texts.

I wasn't in the mood to go back to work, and since I didn't have any of my exclusive clients coming in until tomorrow, I just texted Ali to let her know she was in charge for the rest of the day.

I decided I was going to make some Sloppy Joes tonight since that was Rye's favorite food outside of Mexican, so I needed to stop by the grocery store.

As I looked at different types of hamburger buns, someone called my name. When I glanced over and saw Micah's fine ass, hazel eyes sparkling like stars, I got that same tingle down below from when I'd ran into him back at Rye's school.

"Hey Micah."

"How are you ma?"

"I'm pretty good, you?"

"Great. So I know you said I couldn't take you out, because of your boyfriend, but I'm thinking maybe we can do lunch. Lunch is friendlier than dinner, right? Plus, I think it's low-key fate that we keep running into one another."

Chuckling I said, "We live in the same city, Micah."

"Yeah but we haven't run into each other once since like a year after high school, now all of sudden it's back to back? Come on ma, you know I'm right."

"Uhh..." I looked down at the buns in my hand. "Sure, but I think dinner would be just fine. Make sure it's a place you can afford, because as you can see, I like to throw down."

"I knew that already," he grinned, showing his sexy smile as he lustfully eyes my thick frame. "So let me get your number then." He handed me his phone with the dial screen queued up.

I typed my number in, and then after he called me, I stored his.

See you soon then, Micah."

"Yep. I'll hit you with the details." He stroked his beard and licked his lips as his eyes moved up and down my body again.

If Ryan wanted to play games, then so would I.

CHAPTER THIRTY

Teflon

One week later...

"Ma, how are you feeling?" I touched her small arm and squeezed it.

"I'm doing good enough, Tre'Wayne."

She didn't talk much at all since what happened to my little brother, and I couldn't blame her. Not to mention I felt terrible as hell, and could barely get to sleep at night because the shit I caused. My brother was supposed to be President or some shit, not dead in the grave before he even hit 25.

"Ma, I'm sorry about all of this shit, I really am. I always thought that Torrey would be the one to cause some shit that would be unforgivable, but it turned out to be me." I looked off, shaking my head as I gripped her small hand in mine. She didn't say anything about me cursing like usual. "Believe me when I say if I could go back in time I wouldn't have even come back to Cleveland."

"You can't blame yourself for what that stupid fool did. Your brother had nothing to do with this."

"Yeah but in this game, Ma, nothing is off limits. That's what these niggas do when they wanna hit you where it hurts. They try to sleep with your girl, kidnap your kids, and hurt the people they know you love. Brevin knew how I felt about Thomas, and how proud of him I was."

"It's that woman you call yourself loving." My mother pouted, looking at me briefly before turning away.

"Ma, it's not Tatiana's fault, it's my fault."

"If she would have never thrown herself at you—"

"She did not throw herself at me, Ma! What don't you get about that? I pursued her! I wanted her! She tried to push me away but I wouldn't let up, and that is one thing I don't regret because you're right, I do love her."

"She means more to you than your brother?"

"No, she…" I massaged the bridge of my nose. "No, she doesn't mean more to me than my brother but she's my woman, Ma, and I have to protect her and my baby that she's carrying by any means necessary. Y'all are my family but so is she, and I have to worry about her too."

"Baby? What baby?" My mom snatched her hand from mine.

"Our baby, your grandchild."

"How do you know? Didn't you say she was playing house with that murderer, just before he had my baby killed?"

"Because I just know and I need you to trust me. Speaking of what I need you to do, Ma I have to move you up out of here."

"No. And you said everything was taken care of and I didn't need to worry about someone trying to harm me."

"Yes, and that's true. I didn't want you living here before they shot Thomas, so it has nothing to do with that. I have the means to move you now and I want to."

"We'll see, Tre'Wayne."

"Not a discussion, Ma. I'm gonna have you out of here within the next couple of weeks."

"Kayla is here." She changed the subject.

"I know she called me and told me last week."

"Have you seen her bec—"

"No, I haven't seen her. I really don't want to see her, because I never quite told her about Tatiana and I know this shit is gonna blow the fu— blow up in my face." I fell back against the couch.

"You still love her don't you?"

Turning to look at my mother with a deep frown I said, "What? No. I love Tatiana, trust me," I chuckled. "She has me wondering if I ever loved Kayla," I said more so to myself.

"Hmm. Well Cameron is back there, you should go check on her. I think she's worse off than I am. She won't even go home, and her parents are very bothered by that."

"Aight."

I got up and went towards Thomas' room, before knocking on it lightly. Twisting the knob, I walked inside to see Cameron just sitting there on the bed, with a picture of my brother sitting in her lap.

"Cam, what you doing?" I quizzed, closing the door behind myself. She declined to respond vocally, and just shook her head. "Thomas wouldn't want you like this baby." I sat next to her on the bed.

"How do you know?"

"He's my brother. I knew him before he knew himself. And you know him too."

"He just got back!" She started to cry.

"I know, I know." I leaned her into me and hugged her. "I know he did. Trust me I feel the same damn way."

Cameron was about to have my ass crying too and that wasn't my style at all. I had to hide when I did that shit, most times in the shower where the running water would cover the sound up. My brother had been in Europe for a while, and wasn't even here a damn month before he was gone again.

"I wanna go with him."

"No! No you don't, Cam. Don't you wanna make Thomas happy?" I looked down into her face and she nodded, cheeks drenched. "Then don't hurt yourself baby. He would hate that shit, he really would."

"So what am I supposed to do? I don't wanna eat or go anywhere or do anything. If I stay like this I'm gonna disappear anyway."

We both laughed unintentionally, before she sniffled.

"It's gonna take time. It's cool to be sad, but over time you're gonna do better. Just promise me you won't do anything to yourself. Thomas is gone and the least all of us who loved him can do, is take care of ourselves. Aight?"

She nodded before saying, "Thanks, Tef."

"You're welcome and I'm gonna be checking on you periodically, Cam to make sure you ain't trying to hang yaself or something."

"No I won't," She giggled lightly, wiping her cheeks.

"Good." I kissed her face and then hugged her tightly, before getting up and leaving out. When I got out of my little brother's bedroom, my stomach dropped upon seeing Kayla and my mom on the couch drinking tea. "Kayla," I mumbled, moving slowly into the living room.

"Hey sweetie. I invited her over," my mother smirked softly. Her eyes were still sad though; I could see it.

"Well you guys enjoy your time. I have to get home so I can get some sleep." I darted out and before I was all the way on the porch good, Kayla was calling my name.

"Teflon, so you're just gonna avoid me the whole time?" she closed the front door behind herself. It was dusk, so it was a bit nippy outside.

Sitting down in one of the chairs on my mother's porch I asked, "What you wanna see me for, Kayla?"

She smiled and attempted to sit in my lap but I stopped her, pointing to the chair next to me.

"Wow, last time I checked I was the one who dumped you and should be mad."

"Yeah, you dumped me, which is why I'm confused as to why you constantly try to hit me up or hang out now." I looked at her. "You blew me up while you were in California, and now it's worse because you're here."

She looked good as hell, but she did nothing for me anymore. It was crazy how now that I was with Tatiana, my attraction to other females had this imaginary boundary. It was like my body and mind wouldn't allow me to get pass them being simply pretty or beautiful. Before, only a few seconds would pass before my dick would be telling me to get the number so I could fuck later.

"Look, Tre'Wayne, we've been a part for a while now, and I miss you. You've had time to think and grow, and so have I. Your mother was telling me the other day how much you've matured, and now that Thomas is gone, you need someone."

"Kayla, I have a girlfriend, who I plan to propose to, and who I've already gotten pregnant." When I finished my sentence, I turned to face her.

"What? When?"

"I hate to say it but not long after I moved back."

"Wait, hold up nigga. You fuck me over back in Los Angeles, we break up, you promise me that you won't be fucking with other girls in Ohio, yet now you're telling me you're about to be married and shit?"

"I told you it wasn't likely that I would fall in—"

"No! When I said to promise me that you'd focus on getting better, you're stupid ass said, 'do you honestly think I'd make someone else my girlfriend?'" she mocked me.

"Aight, I may have said that but it didn't happen the way you think it did. I didn't come here, looking to find somebody else Kayla. I literally flew here, got the job I came for, and fell in love."

"Oh so the bitch walked by and you were in love all of a sudden?"

"As crazy as it sounds, that's pretty much how it happened. Regardless of all that though, you and I can't associate with one another anymore. I like what I have with her, and I don't need shit getting in the way."

Shaking her head as tears rolled down she said, "I should have left your ass years ago. I don't know why I stayed so long and now look. But it's cool Tre'Wayne German because when you realize what you've lost, I will be in love with someone else too."

"I hope you do find love." I shrugged and I guess that pissed her off because she started to swing on me. "Chill, Kayla!" I barked, gripping her wrists tightly. "Chill! This ain't worth it! You just said it yourself!"

She yanked her arms from me, barged back into my mother's house and grabbed her purse, ignoring my mom calling her name. She quickly walked to what I assume was a rental because that wasn't her car, and I was sure she flew up here.

"Tre'Wayne, what did you say to her?"

"For once, I told her the truth, Ma."

With that said, I went to my car to leave. I felt bad, but it also felt good to finally get that shit off my chest.

CHAPTER THIRTY ONE

Merce

$\mathcal{I}$ was on my couch trying to get a good nap in since I had about an hour to spare. Shit had gotten really busy ever since Mack got us back hooked up with the connect; this Spanish guy named Mateo who resided in Jamaica.

Between going behind Mack's back to establish our own relationship with Mateo, to putting our chips together to find and purchase a spot to clean our money, I was beat. Not to mention we had to monitor the new traps to make sure niggas weren't on no fuck shit because of their hidden loyalty to Brevin. By saying that, this little ass hour was about to be put to good fucking use.

My damn phone started ringing, and when I saw it was Savannah, I hit ignore. Before I even laid my head back down on the damn pillow, the bitch was calling again. This wasn't no new shit either. She'd been calling and texting me a lot for the past few weeks, and ignoring her wasn't enough to get her ass to go away. I didn't know what had gotten into her because Savannah was never the jealous or stupid as fuck type. She always thought she was too good to chase a man, and it was something I liked about her.

"What?" I roared into the phone, sitting up frowning.

"Why haven't you been answering my calls? I know you seen me calling."

"Sav, what do you want ma? Like for real I don't get it. I don't want you, and for years you made it seem like I was never good enough for you if it had nothing to with making you cum."

"That's not true."

"Like I asked before, what do you want?"

"You."

"Can't have me, I'm taken and even if I wasn't, I wouldn't fuck with you on some serious relationship shit like I've told you before."

"Fuck you, Calvin!"

She hung up and I just placed my phone back onto the coffee table before lying back down. As soon as I started to drift off, I heard keys jingling in my door, before it burst open. Hopping up with my gun, my brows dipped as I watched Sebastian hurriedly try and lock the door before some nigga burst into my got damn crib.

"Aye! Aye what the fuck is going on?" I hollered, clutching my gun tightly in my hand.

WHAM!

The dude punched the shit out of Sebastian, making him fall to the floor, so I walked up and knocked the random nigga ass across the face with the butt of my gun.

"Get the fuck up out of my crib before I send one through yo' head nigga," I hissed, gun pressed to his forehead as blood dripped from his nose.

"Aight, aight." He threw his hands up in mock surrender.

"Who the fuck you work for?" I quizzed as he stood up.

"I don't know. Some niggas named T&D, that's all I know. I swear."

I nodded and then gestured for him to leave, so he raced out. I walked behind him, locking the door, and then I immediately focused my attention on Sebastian's stupid ass.

"What the fuck was that bullshit, Bash?!"

"This dude gave me some fake money, in exchange for drugs. I didn't know the shit was fake." He touched his bleeding lip, and then went to the kitchen to wet a paper towel.

"Come on," I said after watching him for a little bit.

"Where we going?" he frowned.

"You'll see. Bring yo' ass on nigga." I locked my gun in my waist and grabbed my hoodie from the couch to slip it over my head.

I started towards the door and looked over my shoulder to make sure he was following me. He was, and had that same confused ass look on his face. We made it down to my car, and as I sped out onto the street, I could feel his ass glancing at me every now and again.

"Merce, nigga tell me where the fuck you're taking me."

I continued to ignore him, dipping through the streets of Cleveland, anxious to get to my destination. I was tired of this shit, and refused to continue to deal with it. When we pulled up in front of my parents' house, Sebastian snapped his neck to look at me.

"Come on." I got out. I saw he was still in the car, so I tapped on the window and yelled, "Come on!!"

When he got out, I gripped the back of his t-shirt and pushed him closer to my parent's porch. I beat on the door, and waited for one of them to come answer, as Sebastian asked question after muthafucking question.

"Calvin, Sebastian?" my mother unlocked the screen door and opened it, just as my dad came up behind her.

"I ain't here to stay, I'm here to drop him back off to y'all. I'm not doing this shit no more. He's my brother, not my fucking kid, and if he wants to continue to act like one, y'all can be responsible for what happens to him."

"Merce!" Sebastian barked.

"Calvin, what—"

"That's all I wanted to say. I will bring his shit by tomorrow morning. He's y'all responsibility." I turned on my heels and walked off as Sebastian followed me, yapping nonstop while my mother called his name.

I hopped into my whip, cranked it, and then sped off.

Being my brother's keeper was exhausting as hell. I had to let that shit go for good.

***

That night…

"Y'all some bitch ass niggas!" Mack hissed, blood falling from his mouth as he stood there in our warehouse about to die. Garrett's lifeless body was lying next to him.

"Some bitch ass niggas that fooled yo' stupid ass," Teflon commented chuckling. Mack tried to run up, but Teflon punched him in the stomach so hard he collapsed to the ground, hugging his torso and groaning.

Mack was no longer needed. He'd gotten the rest of Brevin's team to trust us and got us connected with the plug, so there wasn't shit else we wanted him for. If he wasn't so untrustworthy, we may have thought about keeping his ass around but that shit was no go.

"I'm wondering if we should make you suffer some more or just get rid of yo' ass," I chuckled, twisting my silencer onto the front of my gun.

"Don't do this shit! Y'all need me," he pleaded, eyes closed.

"Nah, we don't."

PHEW!

I sent one through his head, then nodded for this dude named Fariq to get his body out. Fariq had his own team that was our official clean up crew.

Once they had the body out, Teflon and I left the warehouse to get into his car. Before he was even driving for ten seconds, my phone started to ring and I saw it was Savannah so I hit ignore like always.

"Who was that?" Teflon inquired.

"Savannah."

"Better get that under control," he chuckled.

"Shit, who you telling?"

We made it to our apartment building, and just as we were both about to step out the car, bullets started to fly so we hopped back in and slid down into our seats.

"What the fuck!" Teflon hollered as soon as the bullets ceased.

Before I could respond, we heard screeching tires and loud ass music that sounded like Kid Cudi, distancing.

"I'm guessing that was our competition," I replied, panting heavily.

If it wasn't one thing it was another.

CHAPTER THIRTY TWO

Torrey

$\mathcal{I}$ sped from Teflon's, hoping I'd smoked him and Merce like Diego had paid me to. I didn't want to get too close because my brother might have seen me or worse, started firing back.

Teflon was no punk nigga, and was resilient like a muthafucka; hence his nickname. I'd rather work with him than against him, but since he didn't want that, I had to do what I had to do. Would I miss his ass now that he was possibly dead? I guess, but that nigga ain't never did shit for me but run his fucking mouth about how much better than me he was. It was time I be the only German left anyways. My little brother Thomas was too good for this world, and Teflon was the competition at this point, so he had to exit stage left too.

Pulling up in front of the home I used to fucking share with Audrina, I shut my engine off. Since I touched down we acted more like roommates than a couple. We didn't talk much and when we did, it was mostly arguing because she was trying to tell me what the fuck to do.

Sex wasn't even on the damn table because every time I touched her she bit my damn head off about something. Can you believe that bitch told me she wasn't gon' let me fuck until I could come home with a steady paycheck, prove that I was gonna be faithful, and be a good father? What kind of shit is that? Bitches asked for way too much these days, as if their pussy was the only one around. That's why I'd been breaking off my old hoes left and right to satisfy my needs.

I went to the front door to knock since Audrina wouldn't give me a key, and after a damn hour it seemed, she answered the door with the chain on.

"Audrina, come on and open this shit. It's cold as fuck."

"It's 2am, Torrey."

"So! I had to handle some shit! Let me in! I'm about to fucking freeze out here!"

"I told you if you come home after midnight, it better be because you were getting off a work shift and nothing else."

"I was working!"

"Not illegal shit! Do you wanna go back to jail, Torrey?"

"Open this damn door man! This is my fucking house too!"

"No nigga! You don't pay one bill! Go back to whatever bitch's house that you were just at!"

"I wasn't at no… Fuck!"

She'd slammed the door in my face before I could fully plead my case, and I just stood there listening to her put very damn lock on the door. I turned around and just stared out at the street, wondering what the hell I was about to do. I damn sure wasn't about sleep in my new car that Diego gave me, so I guess I would be going to one of my hoes' house.

I texted Shonda once I got to my car, and she hit me back letting me know that I could stay with her of course.

Fuck Audrina, she could raise our daughter alone. Little girl didn't know me anyway.

***

The next morning… 10:30am…

"Torrey! Torrey!" I felt Shonda shaking me and yelling my name.

"Man Shonda, leave me alone. I'm tired as fuck."

"The police are at the door, and they're looking for you," she whispered, prompting me to sit up quickly.

"What? Uh what they say?"

"They just came to the door asking for you."

"Shit!" I quickly grabbed my boxers from the floor, then my jeans, and put them both on. As I pulled my shirt over my head, I walked to the door where the officers were standing outside, waiting on me.

"Y'all looking for someone?" I asked dumbly.

"Yes, a Torrey German."

"What's the problem officers?"

"Can you step outside for a moment, Mr. German?" The Hispanic officer shot me a quick smile. "We'd just like to have a word with you."

"About what officer?"

"Mr. German, please. This is the last time I'm gonna ask you to step outside for a moment."

Sucking my teeth, I hollered over my shoulder, "Shonda! Bring me my shoes ma!"

When Shonda brought me my shit, I put it on and came outside. The door wasn't even closed good before these niggas slammed me up against the wall.

"Torrey German, you're under arrest for attempted murder…"

"What?" I screamed, face twisted the fuck up as he read me my Miranda rights. I just shot at them niggas last night and I was already getting arrested for it. "Y'all got the wrong man!"

"The shell casings of the bullets match the gun we found in your vehicle," the officer replied, as he and his partner shoved me into the backseat of the patrol car.

Someone had definitely set my ass up. Fuck! This was it for a nigga like me, with a record a 100 miles long…

CHAPTER THIRTY THREE

Groove

Anya and I were leaving the Tower City Center, after buying some shit for my daughter Brin from The Children's Place. I took my baby from Anya, and kissed her fat cheeks a couple times as she smiled and cooed. She was the cutest baby in the damn world, and I knew I would kill any nigga that tried to get anywhere near her.

"Wow," someone called out, and when I looked over I saw Cecily standing there, arms folded with tears streaming her cheeks. "Please tell me that's not your baby."

"Yeah, it is his baby. Did you follow us?" Anya frowned.

Why was this shit happening to me right now? I was legit frozen, not even knowing what the fuck to say.

"I wasn't talking to you, and you're damn right I followed you. Did you know he has a woman already? And a four year old son?"

Anya looked up at me and asked, "Why is she talking like you two are still together, Ryan? You told me you broke up with her."

"Oh really?" Cecily chuckled.

"Yeah I did. I been told you it was a wrap, Cecily," I lied. I figured I had a better chance at keeping Anya at this point so there was no reason for me to fuck that up by pleading with Cecily.

"You did? When did you tell me this because two nights ago you were sleeping next to me! Let me guess he told you he had to work!" Cecily laughed and threw her head back so that her tears wouldn't fall. I felt bad but I had to save whichever relationship I could, and that was obviously with Anya right now.

"I was at work, Cecily. You know damn well I ain't been with you for the longest." I felt like shit as I stared in her face and lied.

After bucking her eyes in disbelief, Cecily turned to look at Anya and said, "I hope you know this nigga is lying." She then looked back to me and shook her head. "You can explain all of this shit to Rye."

I watched her walk away, not even knowing if what the fuck I just did was the right damn thing. I didn't realize I was still staring until Brin started to cry, so I began to rock her until she was calm again.

"Let's go, Anya."

We got to the car, and after buckling Brin in, we were on our way home.

I had been periodically taking a few things from my spot with Cecily, and putting them at Anya's just so I could have equal amounts of shit there, but now I needed to get all my shit from my old spot. And damn, my fucking son.

I wasn't used to not living with him. I'd actually enjoyed being able to kind of live with both him and Brin, but I guess that shit was over with.

When we pulled up to the house, I noticed Anya hadn't said a word the whole damn ride. She was sitting there quietly, as if she were in deep thought.

"You aight?" I asked.

"You lied," she spoke lowly and softly.

"No I didn't, Anya. *She's* lying. I broke up with her and obviously she wasn't too happy, so she's been blowing me up ever since. She fucking followed us!"

"She followed us because she was under the impression that you were still her nigga! That's why!"

"No, because she's jealous! And lower yo' fucking voice! I'm right here! And Brin don't need to here all that fucking yelling!"

"Whatever, Ryan. Just get your shit out of my house, and take it back home. I'm not doing this with you anymore."

"You gon' believe Cecily's ass over me?" I chuckled angrily.

"My gut is telling me that you're lying and I'm gonna trust that."

"You've been nothing but a bitch on the side for the longest, and now all of a sudden you wanna have dignity and morals? Get the fuck out of here. Tell that fake ass story to a nigga who will believe it."

"I don't care if you believe it or not. Just get your shit from my house, and take it wherever the fuck you plan to live because it won't be here. It's over, Ryan." She pulled on the lever to open the door, so I grabbed her arm gently.

"Anya, don't do this shit baby please. I left my family to be with you, and you just gon' throw that shit away?"

"You didn't leave your family to be with me, you lied to your family to be with me. And you played me. You looked me in the eyes and lied, then continued to carry on the lie for weeks. I want a man, Ryan, not a little lying ass boy who can't commit to one woman. I would say to call me when you grow up, but I don't want you to." She yanked her from me and got out of the car.

I sat there, baffled, as she unbuckled Brin from her car seat, and grabbed the baby bag to take it up into the house.

"When can I see her?" I yelled out the window after cranking the car.

"Whenever you'd like. We can put together a schedule," Anya replied, continuing into her home.

"Shit," I shook my head at myself as I backed out of my driveway.

***

That night…

Merce, Teflon, and I were double-checking the day's earnings in the back of the dry cleaners that we'd purchased to clean money in. I could barely focus because of what had transpired earlier today, so I wasn't too much in the mood to do shit but punch a fucking wall.

"Why so upset my nigga?" Merce quizzed. "You look like you're about to cry at any minute."

"How the fuck did I lose two bitches in one day?" I stared off, holding the same band of money that I'd been holding for the past 15 minutes.

"Cecily?" Teflon bucked his eyes.

"Yeah man, *and* fucking Anya. Cecily followed us, and caught me… she caught me with my daughter and Anya."

"Your daughter?" both Merce and Teflon exclaimed.

"Nigga Anya had your baby? Shit is deep with her like that?" Merce added.

"Yes. And I didn't plan that shit, as far as my feelings for her, but it developed naturally, and then Brin came along."

"So what happened when they met? Did they fight?" Teflon inquired.

"Nah they didn't. Anya made me choose a while back and I'd told her I'd chosen her but really I was still with Cecily. Anyway, when Cecily saw us today, she let the cat out the muthafucking bag, but I played her to the left."

"You play who to the left? Cecily?" Merce asked and I nodded. "Nigga, out of those two women, you chose to play Cecily to the left?"

"You're dumb as fuck, Groove." Teflon exhaled and shook his head as he used the money counter.

"I knew it was a wrap with Cecily and I, so I thought why fuck shit up with Anya too? Anyway, Anya ain't fucking with me either because she didn't believe that I'd actually left Cecily. So now I need to find a new place, preferably a house, and I have no woman."

"You just gon' let Cecily go?" Teflon frowned.

"Yeah man, I know her. She's not gonna budge. Neither is Anya. I could see the shit in her face. She was done; they both are."

"I would at least try." Merce shrugged. "Let one of them, whomever you choose, know that you still care and it ain't just nothing to you."

Maybe them niggas were right, but right now I didn't have the energy for that shit. I needed some time.

CHAPTER THIRTY FOUR

Jadynn

"You don't seem as chipper today, Jadynn," my therapist said as I stood up to leave.

This was my last session and honestly it helped a lot. I didn't feel dirty or damaged anymore because of what Russell had done, but I still wanted revenge on him. That didn't look possible though.

"I tried to press charges against Russell for rape."

"Oh, and what happened?" Dr. Larney asked, pausing from putting her legal pad up.

"They basically said it had been too long, and it wouldn't look good because I'd waited. They also said that me waiting forever would also make it seem like I was lying out of jealousy since he'd left me for my sister."

"Wow."

"Yeah."

"Well Jadynn, I would say the only thing to do now is to let that situation go completely. You went through it, you survived it, and now it's time to enjoy your life. Your revenge can be cutting those people out for good. You already told your sister how you felt, so there isn't a need to communicate with her anymore, especially because she doesn't value the relationship at this point. Trust me, her not having you in her life will make her realize what a big mistake she's made."

"True. I guess I shouldn't wish anything bad on her or Russell."

"No you shouldn't, but it's natural if you do. Don't waste your time on them anymore, okay?" I nodded just before she brought me into a hug. "I'm gonna miss you, Jadynn, but you did really well."

"Thanks," I chuckled.

I left the office and when I got down to my car, I sat there for a little bit, letting Dr. Larney's words sink in. She was right. I didn't need to spend anymore time thinking about Russell and Paige, even if it the thoughts did consist of me strangling them. My life was good… great even, and there was no reason I should be moping around about those two.

Paige thought she had it good, but she was pregnant by a good for nothing nigga, who secretly didn't even wanna be with her anymore. And Russell *knew* he didn't have it good, because now he was stuck in a relationship he no longer wanted, with a baby on the way. If you ask me, maybe they were meant for each other. I just hoped my niece grew up to be like her auntie or her grandfather, because Paige, Russell, and my mother were a mess.

Speaking of my mom, I hadn't talked to her since she told me what Russell did wasn't rape. That too had been bothering me, and it was something I needed to let go. Pulling my iPhone out, I dialed my old home number, and waited for my mom to answer.

"Davidsen residence," my mom answered happily. She was the definition of a facade. She loved to pretend everything was honky dory, no matter what.

"Ma, it's Jadynn."

"Oh, hi honey! How are you? You should come over for dinner tonight and—"

"Ma, I'm just calling to let you know that I forgive you and I no longer care about any opinions you may have. I wish you, Paige, and Russell the best, but I just can't be close with you anymore."

"Jadynn, why do you always do this? Ever since you could form full sentences, you've always been so dramatic!"

"Well the good thing then is now you don't have to deal with that. I love you, Ma, but you being in my life on a consistent basis isn't good for me right now."

"Well, when you get out of this little fit that you're throwing for no reason at all, I will be here. You can come by tonight if you want. Paige is coming and I made pie—"

I hung up the phone, shaking my head at her ass always being in denial. It was like what I'd said had went right in one ear and out of the other.

I exhaled happily because today my session had been after work, which meant I could go straight to Merce's apartment now. He told me to be there at 8pm, and since it was already 7:45pm, I just decided to go straight there. I didn't need to change out of my work attire, because he'd seen me in it plenty of times and wouldn't mind.

When I got inside of his building, I made my way to the door and used my key to get inside. Walking in, I saw he'd set up a table with two long stick candles on it. I closed the door behind me, admiring the dark scenery with only the candles to provide light.

Merce came out of the kitchen smiling, before his tall ass pulled me into a hug and kissed my temple. His smooth light skin seemed to have a glow to it, as he stared down at me before pressing his lips against mine.

"What's the occasion?"

"Just want to spend some time with you." He led me to the table, and then pulled a chair out for me. "Let me get your shoes." He dropped down and started to remove my heels.

What the fuck? I thought as I smiled.

"Calvin," I giggled. "Did you cook this?" I lifted the silver top on the platter. There was steak, a lobster tail, shrimp, and mashed potatoes. I was starving too.

"Hell no. I paid some chef nigga to cook all of this."

"Oh," I laughed as he sat across from me.

"How did your last session go?" He asked after we said a prayer over the food. I had to cover my mouth because I was already deep into the buttery mashed potatoes.

"It went well… really well. I don't feel bad about what happened to me anymore. I actually feel strong, as a rape survivor and not a victim."

"Good, because you shouldn't feel bad for what that nigga did to you."

"I know. Pressing charges won't be happening either. Too many complications would be involved because I waited so long. That's what the lawyer told me. And Dr. Larney said to just cut them out of my life now that I've been able to confront them and express myself."

"So no revenge on Russell, huh?"

"Well you beat him up, so that was enough."

"And he hasn't bothered you since right?"

"I umm, no, nope." I quickly lied, not wanting Merce's crazy ass to fly off the handle on me. I didn't care if he beat Russell up again, but I wanted tonight to continue to go smoothly. "Hey, so where is Bash? I haven't seen him here and you haven't complained about him recently."

"I took his ass to my parents house and told them to deal with it. I can't do that shit no more. So from now on, anytime he fucks up, they won't have anyone to blame but themselves."

"Well that's good. Toast to that." I smiled, lifting the flute of champagne, and he followed suit.

There was nothing to complain about at this time, and I was going to enjoy it while it lasted.

CHAPTER THIRTY FIVE

Tatiana

Teflon agreed to come to the mall with me, because I needed a dress for Zeus' event tonight. I'd busted my ass for this shindig, and not only did it need to go perfectly, but I needed to look just as perfect. My belly was growing, so my usual dresses didn't quite fit anymore.

"What do you think of this one babe?" I lifted the dress to show Teflon.

We'd never been shopping together before. He'd usually buy me little things on his own, or some days he would give me cash even though I obviously had my own money.

Anyway, I noticed that I didn't quite like the looks that the women gave him. Handsome was an understatement when it came to Teflon. Smooth, beautiful shade of brown skin, slanted eyes, tall built frame, and he smelled like heaven in a cup. Not to mention he was a great dresser.

"It looks cool but a little short. I told you I need to see that shit on, Tati."

I shook my head at him, and handed him the dress so he could hold it for me while I kept looking. I told him to come to the event, but he said he wasn't sure because he had to take care of a few things. He said he'd maybe come by, and that was good enough for me.

I grabbed about seven dresses, and after trying them on, I chose one but wanted them all, so Teflon bought them for me.

As we left the store, headed for the food court, I spotted Mrs. Williamson and Breeze, walking in the opposite direction, so they were facing us. When we made eye contact, I smiled and waved, and they just shook their heads. Breeze of course rolled her eyes, and whispered something to her mom.

Bitch better whisper.

"That's Brevin's mom and sister," I told Teflon, pointing at them in plain sight so that they'd see.

"That nigga has a sister?"

"Yep."

"Never even mentioned her and she never came by the house or nothing," he replied, still looking. I could see that Breeze liked what she saw as we finally passed one another. It didn't upset me though; in fact it made me want to gloat.

"She moved to Kentucky years ago with her boyfriend, or husband, who knows. He never took her seriously and no one knew why she was following him to another state. She sent a letter claiming they'd gotten married overseas, but Brevin and I didn't believe her."

"Wow."

"I forgot to tell you, some detectives stopped by my job to talk to me about Brevin. I know they sent him, and I'm sure they were upset knowing they had nothing on me."

"Damn, when did this happen?"

"Few weeks ago."

"Why are you just now telling me?" he frowned as we stood in front of the Great Steak and Potato Company.

"I assumed you knew because I gave your cell number to them. And I knew it wasn't a big deal because you told me everything was okay."

He nodded.

"They did call me, but I didn't know they'd talked to you first. And yeah everything is okay, but when shit like that happens, tell me, Tatiana."

"Okay." I sighed. "One of them kind of reminded me of my father."

We placed our order and after he paid, he said, "You told me your adoptive father was alive when I first met you, but you never talk about him and he's never around."

"Well we were close, and got even closer after my mother died, but when I got with Brevin, our relationship started to come apart. I was stupid and in love and my dad just couldn't stand seeing me with him. Eventually I kind of had to choose, and I dumbly chose Brevin. We haven't talked since."

"That's crazy baby. But I know what it's like to be young and thinking you know every damn thing and how your life should be."

"Yeah."

"Maybe you should call him up now that you and Brevin aren't together anymore."

"Yeah… maybe."

We took our food to a table, and sat down to start eating. As Teflon and I started to eat our cheesesteaks, a figure towered over the edge of the table, prompting us both to look up. When I saw Zeus' girlfriend Circe, I placed my sandwich down and exhaled heavily.

"So you have a man of your own I see," she grinned. "A very handsome one at that, which is why I'm confused. What do you want with Zeus?"

"Who the fuck is Zeus?" Teflon frowned, looking Circe up and down. "And back up from being all over my damn food."

Circe stepped back some, wearing a smug expression as she folded her arms.

"Oh, so he doesn't know that you're trying to steal my man?"

"No one is trying to steal your man. He is simply a client and nothing else; trust me. However, he has tried to flirt, but that's something you need to talk with him about." I kept looking back and forth between Circe and Teflon as I spoke. I was nervous as a nigga on a death row.

"What the fuck is going on right now?" Teflon hissed, looking angry as hell.

"I saw purchases for jewelry and flowers on his credit card! When I tracked everything, I found out it was sent to you!" she yelled over the food area.

"Tef, her boyfriend is a client at the PR agency and it's his party that we're doing tonight. He bought me a few things but I didn't keep them I swear. I told him to back off, and that I was in a relationship. I even told him about the baby, which you know I wanted to keep quiet about."

"You need to—"

"No, you need to take yo' ass on with all that yelling and shit!" Teflon barked at Circe. "She don' told yo' ass what it was, now you need to go confront that nigga before we have some fucking problems."

After frowning down at me for a while, Circe finally said, "Just stay away from him." She pranced off and I looked at Teflon who shook his head at me.

"I swear I told him."

"You should have told *me*. Stop keeping secrets Tatiana, or we not gon' make it. I'm telling you right now."

"I know and I won't, I'm sorry. I just knew you'd try to approach him."

"And I will."

"Teflon."

"Tatiana." He stared deeply into my eyes. I knew there was no changing his mind so I went back to eating my food.

✳✳✳

The party...

The opening of Zeus' restaurant called Zeus, had been in full swing for the past hour. Everyone that was invited had showed up, and so far people were loving the food; we'd have to get the food critic's opinion later after he wrote about it. But so far, tonight was perfect, and everyone had a smile on their faces.

"We did good," Jadynn cheesed, sipping her glass of champagne as she stood next to Merce, surveying the place. We'd all rode in one car, since it was no point in hunting for two or three parks for the night.

"I know right."

"So much damn gold," Merce looked around.

"Well we're gonna take a break and try some of the food. Are you gonna come?" Jadynn started to lead Merce away.

"Yep, just have to check on a few people and then I will be over to you guys' table."

I moved through the restaurant just to make sure that everyone looked please, and I ended up bumping into Zeus.

"Just the girl I was looking for," he grinned.

"Zeus, I've been meaning to talk to you."

"Me first." He pulled a red rose from behind his back, and there were some diamond studs sitting inside. "A thank you gift."

"Zeus, look this is the last time I'm gonna tell you, I'm not interested. And your girlfriend popped up on my boyfriend and I earlier, going off about you. I do not want those problems, especially behind a man I have no interest in. If you're not happy in your relationship, you need to go find some insecure ass hoe who is willing to lie on her back and be your side chick because it ain't me. My boyfriend is already wanting to beat your ass, so it's best you stop while ahead." With that said, I shoulder checked him, more like arm checked since he was way taller than me, and made my way around the restaurant.

Once I was sure everyone was okay and enjoying the food and atmosphere, I went to find Jadynn, Merce, and Suzanne who I'd invited. I told her once Teflon and I moved, she could come work for us, so now she was staying in Teflon's spare bedroom. Prior to, she was living out of a hotel, something I had no idea she was doing.

By the time it was midnight, the party started to come to an end as people left. Soon enough, it was only Jadynn, Eddie, Merce, Zeus, Circe who popped up out of nowhere, and me. As all of us chatted, the door opened and entered Teflon looking like a model in his gray tweed suit from Banana Republic. Nodding his head to say what's up to Merce, he scoped the scenery.

"Zeus?" Teflon walked right up to Zeus, eyebrows furrowed.

"Oh shit," Jadynn mumbled as Merce chuckled.

"Tre'Wayne," I came to him, nervous about his plans as I adjusted my purse strap.

"Oh you must be Tatiana's boyfriend. She's told me so much ab—"

WHAM!

Zeus went flying across a few tables, knocking the silver wear down, and crushing a couple wine glasses when he hit the floor on his back. Everyone stood there in disbelief, as Teflon grabbed my hand, and led me out of the restaurant.

"Tre'Wayne!" I laughed as we walked to his car.

"Told you I was gonna get at him."

"I know but dang," I chuckled.

He stopped walking and picked me up, so I wrapped my legs around his waist, and my arms around his neck.

"I love you, Tef."

"I love you too baby." He kissed my lips a few times, as we continued to his car.

CHAPTER THIRTY SIX

Cecily

A week and a half later...

"Wow, so it's really over?" Tatiana frowned. She and Jadynn were over, finally getting the scoop on why Ryan and I were no longer.

"Yes. I mean I was done when I saw him with the baby. I knew it was his because the little girl looked just like him. But when he tried to pretend for that girl, I was really over it."

"Has he called?" Jadynn inquired.

"Just to find out when he can get Rye. Other than that we don't talk."

I admit it was hurtful that he hadn't tried, but I was moving on to other things, or at least trying to. Micah and I had been out a few times, and the more time we spent together, the more I wondered why I ever left him to be with Ryan. I mean I know why, but my logic back then was dumb. Ryan was no good, but that was what attracted me to him. And I felt that because someone that was as fine as him liked me,

I had to jump on it.

Micah was so much better though. He was good to me back in high school and he's even better now. Only reason I wouldn't go back and change my decision is because of my son. I loved Rye more than anything, even though he was a part of Ryan's trash ass.

"Dang, I wonder if he's with her," Tatiana stared off.

"No. I ran into her the other day at the grocery store. We got to talking and she told me Ryan was trying and had finally given up."

"Niggas," Jadynn sucked her teeth.

I was sad Ryan and I had ended, but I would be perfectly fine even if I didn't kind of have Micah right now.

The three of us relaxed for hours, watching movies, eating, and just talking. Around 7pm, there was a knock at the door, and I knew it was Ryan because Rye was due back to me tonight. Currently, I had Rye from Sunday night to Thursday morning, and Ryan had him from Thursday evening to Sunday night.

"That's Ryan," I said, getting up. Both Jadynn and Tatiana's eyes were wide as hell as they prepared to leave, making me chuckle.

"Hey boo!" I smiled down at Rye as he hugged my leg. "Did you have fun with your daddy?"

"Yes! We went to the park, stayed up late, ate pizza, and watched scary movies!" he explained excitedly as both Ryan and I followed him to his bedroom.

I waved bye to Tatiana and Jadynn in passing, who also spoke to Ryan and Rye, before I said, "Sounds like fun. Go get your pajamas out because it's time for a bath, okay?"

"Okay! Bye daddy!" he exclaimed, as Ryan and I left out of his bedroom.

"Aye, Cecily, let me talk to you." Ryan grabbed my wrist, stopping me from going into the bathroom to start the bathwater.

"What?" I frowned, pulling away.

"I'm sorry about everything, and I just feel like we have way too much history together to just let shit go."

"Ryan, you cheated on me, had a baby on me, and then acted like we hadn't been together in front of your side chick. Do you honestly think I can forgive you?"

"If you love me."

"Not enough love in the world, Ryan."

KNOCK! KNOCK!

I started towards the front door, and Ryan followed right behind me.

"Cecily, you don't even want to try! I love you and I'm here, trying!"

"Oh because Anya wouldn't take you? Yeah, I ran into her and she let me know that you'd been trying and failing for weeks. So I guess you thought old baby mama Cecily would take you back now right?"

"All the shit I did for you! If it wasn't for me you would have still been some insecure ass bitch with no money and no fucking goals!"

I nodded slowly at him with my eyes bucked, before looking out the peephole to see Micah was here.

I opened the door for him.

"Hey baby." I leaned up and kissed Micah's lips. I then turned to Ryan and frowned, "Like I said Ryan, I'll pass on you."

There was so much egg on his face as he looked from me to Micah and from Micah to me over and over, that I wanted to laugh. He finally slipped past us both, and stormed off.

"Everything alright?" Micah walked in, closing the door behind himself.

"Perfect. Make yourself comfortable while I go give Rye his bath."

Micah nodded and went to the fridge to get a beer.

Yep, Ryan could kick rocks.

CHAPTER THIRTY SEVEN

Merce

Jadynn and I got invited to my parents' home to have dinner and so they could meet her. I was gon' say no at first, but I wanted to make sure my brother was good, and I did want my peoples, outside of Sebastian and Teflon, to know my girlfriend.

Shit went well, because my parents behaved themselves, and Sebastian seemed to have turned over a new leaf. He had the nerve to be enrolled in school, but it was only because old boy that I pulled a gun on, had caught up to him and jumped him. I wasn't even going to come after the boy because Sebastian needed to learn. Not only was he not about the street life, but also he needed to do better for himself, and definitely better than I'd done for myself. And even though I'd gotten sucked into this street shit, I was gon' be in it forever.

Teflon, Groove, and I were opening a legit business together, and hopefully it was just the start of many more.

"That was nice. I was scared at first but they turned out to be okay.

I almost didn't recognize Sebastian," Jadynn chuckled, as we walked to my car hand in hand.

"Shit me either but I hope it lasts. He needs to do better than me."

As I opened the passenger door for Jadynn, I pulled my phone from my pocket. I'd had it on Do Not Disturb where only the people in my favorites could get through, so I hadn't checked it. I saw I had a text from Savannah that she sent about three hours ago. The picture was of Jadynn and Russell sitting down together outside of what looked like Starbucks.

"Aye, what is this?" I asked Jadynn once I was in the driver's seat.

After staring at the picture for the longest she replied, "He umm, he came to talk to me and I basically told him how I felt. I told you I confronted him!"

"No, you said I confronted *them!* I thought you meant your mama and Paige. I didn't know you were calling his ass up and scheduling meetings!" I barked, cranking my car and making a quick ass U-turn.

"I didn't! He followed me there and tried to talk, but I went in on his ass!"

"Aight."

At the red light I text one of these smart ass dudes that we'd officially hired to find shit and people for us. I'd used him to find Russell before, and I needed him to do it again.

"What does aight mean?"

"Nothing, Jay."

"Whatever."

The ride was silent and when I got to her apartment, I stopped to let her out. She stared at the side of my face for a moment, and then sucked her teeth before getting out, calling me all kinds of names.

While I waited for that information on Russell, I drove to Savannah's house because I was tired of her ass. She'd been doing little shit here and there, thinking nobody knew it was her. From throwing shit on Jadynn's car, which I didn't know about until recently, to leaving a dead bird on her doorstep, Savannah had been wilding. Jadynn just thought the bird incident were some bad as neighborhood kids, but I knew that it was a part of the new jealous ass Savannah.

I parked in front of her house, and rushed up the steps to beat on the door. I got no answer, so I went around back because I knew she always forgot to lock the back door. Once inside the house, I darted to her bedroom, burst in, and chuckled lightly when I saw her giving some nigga top.

"Aye, man I didn't know she had a nigga." The dude threw his hands up, as Savannah covered herself with a sheet.

"Get out of my house!" she yelled.

I walked up without saying a word, and snatched her ass up by her hair. I then pulled her threw the house as she swung on me and screamed, before I flung her naked ass outside. She tried to run back in, so I grabbed her by the hair again and pressed my gun under her chin. No one could see my piece but us, and her ass froze up like a possum playing dead at the feel of that cold steel.

"No no, no! Please Calvin, please." She started to cry, not caring that she was ass naked for the street to see.

"Didn't I tell you to leave me and my girl the fuck alone?"

"Yes, yes and I am I promise. I won't do anything else!"

"I think I should kill you."

"Don't! Calvin please don't. I swear I'm done. That was just the last thing."

"One more fuck up, Sav, and I'm going to kill you. Look at me. I will murder yo' ass."

She nodded repeatedly as tears ran down her cheeks. I tossed her to the ground and she began hyperventilating while trying to cover her breasts.

As I turned to walk to my car, I saw old boy she'd had in the bed, hop in his whip shirtless, and peel off. I had to chuckle and shake my head at his scary ass.

***

Around 2am...

I stood across the street and watched Russell kill off a bottle of liquor while still in his car. I was leaning up against a tree just waiting. He'd just come from work, and clearly he didn't want to be home because of how long he sat in his whip.

He finally got out of the car, and as soon as he turned his back, I walked quietly across the street. Once we were both on the sidewalk at the same time, I ran up behind his ass.

"Didn't I say to leave Jadynn alone?" I gritted in his ear, holding him tightly in a headlock so that he couldn't breathe or scream.

I let him struggle for a little bit, before I brought my knife around and slit his fucking throat. He dropped to the door and started twitching for a bit, and once he stopped, I booked it around the corner, hopped on my bike, and sped off.

It seemed like it took forever on this bike, but once I got a couple blocks from Jadynn's, I ditched it, and then walked the rest of the way.

When I got in her apartment, I took a hot shower, changed into a pair of boxers I had over there, and then got in bed behind her.

"Hey," she whispered, placing her arm on top of mine as I kissed her shoulder.

"Hey."

"I'm sorry I didn't tell you."

"It's fine." I hugged her body tighter into mine. "I love you."

She turned onto her back and looked at me before saying, "I love you too."

CHAPTER THIRTY EIGHT

Almost a month later...

"This was your surprise?" Tatiana frowned as we stood inside of an empty old restaurant. There was dust everywhere pretty much.

"Yeah, what do you think?"

"Well, umm I don't know. What the hell is it?" she quizzed, making me laugh.

"It's a restaurant, but I'm gonna fix it up and shit, make it look good. Told you I always wanted to do this shit."

"I know. So how much is this all going to cost?"

"Well the renovations that Merce, Groove, and I want, are gonna cost about $150,000 but I think it's worth it. Do you?"

"Yeah I do. It's a great location. A lot of traffic around here and you know once it's all ready to go, you can hire me."

"Hire? Damn, so I can't get any services for free?" I moved closer to her, and leaned down to peck her lips a few times.

"It depends."

"On?"

"How well you perform tonight." She winked and turned around to walk the restaurant. I just watched, admiring how beautiful she was with that pregnancy glow, until someone knocking on the window got my attention.

I looked over to see what looked like Mack's bitch, Gloria. She was wearing a tight ass dress, and her belly was small but obvious.

Opening the front door I said, "What?"

"Hey Tef, I was wondering if I could talk to you for a moment." I looked up and down the block, making sure it wasn't a set up, then nodded my head so she could continue. "Yeah, so I was wondering if I could borrow some money to pay the note on Mack's and my house. He's ran off somewhere, and the bills are due. If I can't pay I'm gonna have to live with my mom and she's in an apartment."

"So? What the fuck I look like to you? We ain't spoke two words to one another, Gloria."

"I know, but if you do something for me, I can do something for you."

"Watch it bitch!" Tatiana yelled from behind me. I didn't even know her ass was listening.

"Oh, hey Tati!"

"Don't 'hey Tati me."

"Look Gloria, I don't know what the fuck to tell you."

"Please Tef—"

I closed the door in her face, and went back to looking around the restaurant with Tatiana. About 10 minutes later, my mother was knocking on the glass so I let her in.

"Hey sweetie." She hugged me, before feasting her eyes on Tatiana. "Hi, Tatiana."

"Hello, Mrs. German."

"So what did you call me here for, Tre'Wayne?" my mom questioned.

"Well, I wanted the two most important women in my life to see this new business venture before it gets all fixed up."

"You're finally opening a restaurant?" my mother beamed, scanning the place with her eyes.

"Yep. But Ma, I also want you to be nice to Tatiana. I love her, she's having my baby, and I'm gonna ask her to marry me."

My mom exhaled heavily and then said, "I'm sorry for what I said at the repast, I was just upset and sad. I know you don't deserve to be blamed for what that ex of yours did. And I admit I wanted him to be with Kayla but I guess that was because I was used to her. However, I have to thank you for making my little boy become a man because for the longest, I thought he'd grow old alone with a beer belly and hearing loss."

She and Tatiana burst into laughter.

"Why do I have to lose my hearing, Ma?" I asked and they both laughed harder.

"I understand, Mrs. German. I probably would have reacted the same way but trust me I love your son very much, and he's smart so he wouldn't have even given me the time of day if he thought I was bad news."

"I know and honey, please call me Tam. I guess we should hug now."

"Okay, Tam," Tatiana smiled as they moved closer and embraced.

"Well now that I have your approval finally…" I reached into my pocket to pull out the diamond ring I'd bought a couple weeks ago. Getting down on my knee, I looked up at Tatiana who already had glazed eyes. "People don't believe me but from the first time I saw you Tatiana, I knew I wanted you to be my wife. I know it sounds cliché, but it's the truth I swear. So will you do me the honor?"

She nodded as my mother took picture after picture, flash blinding me like a muthafucka. I should have never gotten her ass a cellphone.

"Yes, Tef," Tatiana finally responded as I slid the ring on.

Standing up, I pulled her into me and kissed her slowly, thumbing the few tears that slid down her supple cheeks.

"I love you, Tati."

"I love you too, Tre'Wayne."

***

A few days later…

I sat in the corner of the dark hotel room, dressed down in an all black suit from Banana Republic. I was taking my baby to dinner tonight, but I had to handle some shit real quickly. As I slipped my phone back into my coat pocket, I retrieved my gun from my waist with my gloved hands.

Diego entered his hotel and sighed, taking his jacket off before going into the bathroom. Standing up, I followed him, and as soon as he flicked the lights on, I closed the bathroom door and pressed my gun to his head.

He panicked as he spotted my shoe covers and gloves.

"Teflon, you're gonna regret this."

"Nah, I don't think so. See you got away with killing your own damn brother, and you should have left it at that, but nah you had to come to *my* city, convince my stupid ass brother to shoot at me… yeah I knew it was him. Nigga loves Kid Cudi and forgot to turn his music down when he shot at us."

"I didn't convince him—"

"You did. I know you gave him the car he used, and the niggas that were supplying the streets were named T&D, so stop it. Then you got him arrested and thrown back in jail and because of his record, they're most likely gonna give him life."

Don't get me wrong, I was pissed my brother tried to kill me for a few dollars, but I was more pissed that Diego had played him.

"He did—"

PHEW! PHEW!

Diego fell back into the bathtub, so I put my gun back up and left the room. Standing outside of the hotel building was one of the camera operators of the hotel. He'd shut it off for me, so I paid him $1000 before getting in my car and heading to pick up Tatiana and go eat.

I could finally stop sleeping with both eyes open, and only sleep with one open. Being in this game, I would always have to look over my shoulder but not as frequently, thank God.

EPILOGUE

Tatiana German

Four years later…

"Mom! Mom!" Tre'Wayne Jr. ran into the bedroom. He loved to call my name twice and it was adorable. I just wished he still called me mommy.

"Yes baby?" I quizzed as I fluffed out my hair in the mirror.

All of our friends were here, because it was my twenty-ninth birthday party. It felt good to be twenty-nine because my life was finally what I'd always wanted it to be. I had a wonderful husband, a beautiful son, a daughter on the way, and now my own PR Company that I co-owned with Jadynn. I had even gotten back close to my father, but he'd moved to Illinois years ago and I didn't know, so we couldn't spend time together like I'd wanted.

My life was a complete 180 from the one I'd had with Brevin years ago. That nigga would have probably killed my ass by now. It felt good to be free from him, his mama, and his stupid ass sister Breeze, even though she wasn't present for most of our relationship. Pretty much anything dealing with Brevin was wiped clean from my life. The simple thought about the fact that I had actually tried to stay with him, made me shudder.

"Are you done yet? I'm supposed to bring you down to the party!" TJ smiled, looking just like his handsome father.

"Okay, alright. I'm ready."

I put my hand into his little one, and then we came out of the bedroom. Teflon and I lived in a big beautiful two-story home in Ohio City, and he let me decorate everything to my liking except one of the dens, which was his relaxing room.

TJ and I descended the stairs, and then I let him lead me to the back room where everyone was standing, waiting for me. All my close friends were here, which wasn't too many, and there my husband was with his fine self, holding a cake. He grinned widely upon seeing me, as everyone shouted happy birthday.

"Thank you," I shrieked, hugging Jadynn who rushed me.

"You don't look a day over twenty-one, Tati." She kissed my cheek.

Jadynn and Merce had gotten married two years ago, and had been trying ever since to have a baby. She was finally pregnant, and we were only a month apart so our kids would be the same age. Even better was that she too was having a girl.

Her sister Paige was devastated to find out someone had murdered Russell, but that only lasted for about a month. She was now supposedly in love with this fine ass white guy, and had moved to North Dakota with him and her daughter Penelope. Jadynn couldn't leave her mother behind liked she'd planned, so they did talk, but Jadynn just didn't value her opinions like she used to. She finally realized that her poor mother lived in and never planned to leave Fool's Paradise.

"Happy birthday beautiful," Merce smiled and hugged me, before draping his arm around Jadynn.

Merce and Teflon's Waffle House had taken off, and it was like the prime breakfast spot in Cleveland. I was so happy for Teflon, because he'd followed through with something so risky and scary aka, getting into the restaurant business. The restaurant was really nice, and a big change from the dusty haunted house looking spot it was four years ago.

"Thanks, Merce." I grinned.

Teflon came up and kissed me deeply, before whispering a happy birthday and then delivering another peck. I was hot and ready that quickly, and watched him with lust in my eyes as he scooped TJ up and tickled him. Rye came up, and he and TJ rushed off somewhere in the room once Teflon put him down.

"Hey lady!" Cecily grinned, holding hands with Micah.

Their love story was sweet because they were high school sweethearts who'd gotten separated and came back together. They'd gotten married, but hadn't had any babies yet. Cecily said she wanted to wait until her second nail shop was up and running. I was proud of her, and couldn't wait until the grand opening of the new one, which was in a month. She'd hired Jadynn and I for PR services too.

As for Groove, who was currently coming up to me, arm around some girl, he was still a player and didn't want to settle down. He was a great father to Brin and Rye, but he had no plans on settling down he said.

"Happy birthday, beautiful," Groove smiled. He and Cecily didn't talk much unless it was regarding Rye. It was sad to see because I remember when they used to be so in love, but Ryan had done one of the worst things you could do to your woman. I applauded both Anya and Cecily for leaving his ass, even though I loved him.

For the rest of the night we danced, ate, and had non-alcoholic and alcoholic champagne. I partied hard for a pregnant woman, and I loved every moment of it.

"Thank you for everything, Tre'Wayne," I whispered to him as I sat in his lap, feeling his erection grow under as he groped my thigh, while I watched everyone have a good time.

"Of course baby, I got your back."

"And I yours." I kissed him, caressing the side of his face.

FIN

Join my mailing list to get a notification when Shvonne Latrice has another release!

Text **SHVONNE** to **66866** to join!

www.ingramcontent.com/pod-product-compliance
Lightning Source LLC
Chambersburg PA
CBHW061345310726
48974CB00001B/200